I0668990

Also by Seconde Nimenya

Evolving Through Adversity
A Hand to Hold
A Leader's Companion Workbook

For a complete list of Seconde Nimenya's products, services, and to order any of the books and audios listed above, or for information on her workshops, speaking events and other programs, please contact:

Seconde Nimenya
info@SecondeNimenya.com
www.SecondeNimenya.com

PRAISE FOR
EVOLVING THROUGH ADVERSITY

"This book is great and so inspiring. I can't even imagine moving halfway across the world and readjusting to a new culture. I really enjoyed reading *Evolving Through Adversity*."

— **Tyler R. Tichelaar, Ph.D. award-winning author of**
The Best Place

"If you are looking for a resource to give you hope and for overcoming all life's adversities, then, start here!"

— **Patrick Snow, international best-selling author of**
Creating Your Own Destiny

"What a gift! Written by an extraordinary woman who, through much adversity, finds incredible potential within herself. This book is filled with lessons of perseverance and hope, beneficial to everyone."

— **Susan Friedmann, CSP, international best-selling**
author of *Riches in Niches*

"Growing up in a culture completely unlike our own, we learn about the experiences of a little girl whose pain and history shaped her into who she is today."

— **H.C. "Joe" Raymond, author of**
Embracing Change from the Inside Out

"*Evolving Through Adversity* is an example of how we can't love and honor others, without first loving and honoring ourselves. Love comes from within, and this book teaches us how to find it."

— **B. Imei Hsu, LMHC and Founding Counselor of**
Seattle Direct Counseling

PRAISE FOR
A HAND TO HOLD

"If you're tired of reading fantasy romance novels with impossibly handsome hunks and unrealistic heroines, then try something a lot closer to reality. Wouldn't you rather read about real people with real problems anyway, and learn how they overcome those problems?"

— **Tyler R. Tichelaar**

"Truly an incredible and amazing inspirational book! In Seconde's *A Hand To Hold*, I felt a spirit of humanity. This is an inspirational fiction book that will make you laugh and cry, and in the end, leaves you feeling that no matter your race, gender, cultural background, all people want the same thing: to express our uniqueness, which is ultimately our purpose; and in order to do so, we must never ever give up hope."

— **Jessica Davis**

"A story filled with heart and soul. In *A Hand To Hold*, the author uses the power of story to imprint dramatic pictures to move, touch, inspire and emotionally connect us to her forceful and robust characters. Despite the adverse situations they encounter, we're left with the powerful universal message to never ever give up, no matter what happens to us in life."

— **Susan Friedmann**

"Wow! Just Amazing is an understatement for this book! I am in awe by the creative performance of this novel. It's not only a story to read, but a revolution in the making. *A Hand To Hold* is truly inspiring, raw and the imagery is powerful."

— **Amazon Customer**

A HAND TO HOLD

SECONDE NIMENYA

International award-winning author of
EVOLVING THROUGH ADVERSITY

A Hand to Hold
Copyright ©2016 & 2018 by Seconde Nimenya

This book is a work of fiction. Names, characters, places, incidents, and other events are the product of the author's imagination, and are used fictitiously. Any resemblance to actual persons, living or dead, events, or locations is entirely coincidental.

All Rights Reserved. No part of this book may be reproduced or transmitted in any form or shape, or by any means, electronic, mechanical, including photocopying, recording, or by any information storage or retrieval system, without prior written permission of the author or publisher, except where permitted by law.

Address all inquiries to:
Seconde Nimenya
info@SecondeNimenya.com
Website: www.SecondeNimenya.com

Edited by Tyler Tichelaar
Cover & Interior Design by Fusion Creative Works
Author Photo by Sandra Hixon-Matthews

Library of Congress Control Number: 2015920035

Nimenya, Seconde
A Hand to Hold/ Seconde Nimenya.
p.cm.

Print ISBN: 978-1-943164-52-3

Published by Aviva Publishing
Lake Placid, New York
www.AvivaPubs.com

Fiction/Romance   I. Title.
Manufactured in the United States of America
First Edition

For book orders: www.SecondeNimenya.com

To my family,

Thank you for being there when I needed
a Hand to Hold.

I love you.

CHAPTER 1

Adina quickly surfed the news channels, looking for the weather report, and landed on Al Roker on NBC. The weather map showed rain all over New York State, so Adina decided to wear her black raincoat. After she finished brewing her coffee and packing her lunch, she went to wake up her son to get him ready for middle school. Haile was still in a deep slumber at 7:20 a.m., despite always setting his alarm clock to wake him at 7:00 a.m. Adina gently shook him, but he only stirred. Then Adina started her routine, massaging his back as he always asked her to do. Haile told his mother that the massage helped him to awaken faster. Every morning, Haile just turned on his stomach, so his mother could rub his back. This was always the time when Adina felt like a tyrant— leaving her only son home alone to send himself off to school. Fortunately, the public school Haile attended on Roosevelt Island was less than a mile away from where they lived on Main Street, in the extension of New York City's Manhattan neighborhood.

Geneva, Adina's middle child, had already left for school earlier since she was in high school, and Bella, the oldest, was a junior at Syracuse University. When Haile had turned eleven, he had assured his mother he was big enough to stay home on his own so his mother could catch the early morning aerial tramway to the subway that would take her to Brooklyn at the Media Express Company where she worked. Haile was a very independent boy, and had been so from the moment he was born. At his birth, unlike most babies, he had surprised everyone when he started sucking his mother's breast milk on the first attempt without any assistance. At five months, he had started crawling, and he could hold his spoon and feed himself at six months old. At exactly eleven months, Haile was walking steadily, without holding on to the furniture. At four years old, Haile had made his first omelet to everyone's amazement, which had horrified his mother, who worried he could get burnt. He did sometimes, but fortunately, with only minor booboos.

Everyone was always amazed by how mature Haile was. When his parents got divorced, Haile was nine years old. Sometimes, he wanted to take on more manly work, so his mother wouldn't feel alone or burdened. But Adina, always protective of her children, often had to draw the line with Haile, which could lead to an argument.

"You always treat me like a baby!" Haile angrily told his mom one day when they had returned from the store and she wouldn't let him carry the heavy boxes of groceries into the house.

"But, sweetie, I don't want you to break your back; you're still growing," Adina replied. "You need to clean up your room instead; have you seen how messy your room is?"

"Mom, don't change the subject; you always do that!" Then Haile would retreat to his room and slam the door so loudly that his mother was afraid it would fall off the wall one day.

Although Haile wanted to prove he was grown by doing work beyond his age, cleaning his room was far from being one of his favorite chores. Sometimes, his room would stay messy for so long that his mother ordered him to clean it up, threatening to take away all his PlayStation games. But what best motivated him was when Adina disconnected the TV and Internet cables, so he couldn't watch TV or play games on the computer. That punishment seemed to be quite efficient, so Adina resorted to it more than once. The same went with his sisters who liked to play music on YouTube. They knew better than to push their mother's last nerve. The Internet cable could disappear for days, even weeks, if the kids hadn't finished their chores. So quite often, Bella and Geneva blamed their little brother for the missing cables, and they were the ones who ordered him to clean his room so their mother could reinstate the Internet and cable TV.

Now with Bella in college, Adina was still working hard at letting go of her oldest daughter. Bella was like a second mom to her siblings, and they actually listened to her more than to their mother. Bella said it was because their mother spoiled Geneva and Haile and didn't discipline them as much as she had her. This was true to some extent.

"That's because you're my firstborn, sweetie! I didn't have any experience in raising kids; I was almost a kid myself when I had you," Adina said one day when the conversation came up again.

"Mom, you were twenty-four when you had me!" Bella replied, rolling her eyes and causing all three kids to burst out laughing. Adina feigned shock on her face.

"So? That's young! You think at twenty-four I knew what a baby would entail?" Adina defended herself.

"I am having my first child when I'm twenty-two!" Haile announced.

"What? Twenty-two!" said Adina, "That's a baby! A baby having another baby? How are you going to provide for your family?"

"I'm getting married at twenty-six and never having children because I will be a career woman," Geneva declared.

"What? Having no kids? Are you depriving me of grandchildren?" Adina asked.

"Yep, Mom," Bella proclaimed, "you can count on the rest of us, your two sweet children, because Geneva will always be the same selfish person she's always been."

"I'm not selfish!" Geneva replied.

"That's not a nice thing to say about your sister, Bella," Adina reprimanded; she could see that Geneva's feelings were hurt. Although Bella was only kidding, whatever she said seemed to have a big impact on her sister's self-esteem. Geneva wanted her sister's approval in everything, and she was always upset whenever Bella disagreed with her. Adina didn't want any of her children feeling bullied, especially by a sibling. She had grown up as an only child, so she didn't really know how siblings interacted with each other. Sometimes, arguments could drive a wedge between the two sisters. But unlike her mother, Geneva was a conflict handler. Occasionally, she gave a piece of her mind to her sister, which caused a cat fight between them. But despite sisterly fights, the three kids loved each other and were Adina's source of joy.

· · · ·

That Thursday, when Adina arrived at work, she wasn't prepared for what lay ahead of her. She worked in the advertising company's accounting department, so she started her routine work with Excel spreadsheet reports, trying to resolve discrepancies built up from the last six years. Previously, most of the accounting reports had been done manually, but now, due to recent growth, the company was upgrading to a new accounting system. In the last ten years, the organization had grown from a mere six employees to a little over 200 at the headquarters level, in addition to people in field offices throughout the world. Adina's job was to fix accounting errors made in the last six years. At the same time, she had multiple deadlines for current reporting for at least another dozen reports. The company had received a lot of public funds from grants, which demanded a lot of forms and reports.

That day, the report Adina had been working on for days was once again rejected by her manager, Patty Monaghan. Forced to redo the report, Adina plugged in her earphones so she could listen to music while she worked all morning and part of the afternoon on the same report. She couldn't figure out what was wrong with the report because all the numbers on it seemed to balance. But she knew better than to ask her manager for clarification because she was newly hired and still in her three-month probation period before she could become a full-time employee. Patty had already told her, when she'd barely been there two months, that if she didn't improve her work, she would be let go when the probation period ended.

Since starting this job, Adina had shown interest in her work, but something always seemed off balance. She felt as if she were on trial and not allowed to make any mistakes from day one. Every Excel error resulted in scolding and condescending remarks from Patty and the coworker who had trained her. Each time Adina made a mistake, her trainer would run to Patty to report how stupid Adina was. After a month and half, Adina was under constant watch. She knew that each mistake she made was recorded by Patty, who likely needed documentation to justify firing her.

The job was tenuous with many details, and it quickly became unsatisfying and a source of anxiety for Adina. She knew she wasn't the kind of person who performs well under pressure, but she made up her mind to do her very best to improve her performance. And she did, in her own way. She took work home on Fridays to work on over the weekends, so she could be ahead on Mondays. When one day, Maria, the receptionist who had been with the company since its launching, commented on Adina's dedication in front of Patty, Adina started feeling she might keep her job after all; she so desperately needed it.

After she got married, Adina had spent most of her time raising her kids, not pursuing a career. This was her first job after her divorce, and God knew she needed it to provide for herself and her three children.

The day Adina's three-month probation was to end, she felt very nervous, but by three o'clock, her tension had started to lessen when no one had approached her. Adina was now deep into her Excel spreadsheets when Patty, accompanied by Brad Stipp, the HR director, came into her office, and closed the door behind them. Brad was in his early sixties, but he looked ninety; everybody called him Mr. Stipp, which made him seem even older than he was. He was bald and had a white moustache that made him look like he had forgotten to wipe the milk off his mouth. No one ever wanted him around; he seemed to suck all the energy from the room with his sad face that looked as if somebody had just died.

Now he was in her office. Adina knew that couldn't be good news! But Adina was also a somewhat optimistic person. She actually had empathy for Mr. Stipp; he seemed to be misunderstood in his life. For a minute, Adina thought Patty and Mr. Stipp might have decided to lift the probation period and offer her full-time employment. *Hey, since when is hoping a sin?* Adina thought to herself. But Patty wasted no time announcing the object of her and Mr. Stipp's visit.

"This is about your job. We need details. This job is detail-oriented. You have missed the details many times, and I have constantly had to review your work, and I am tired of that," Patty said, waving about a letter before she put it on the desk in front of Adina. Adina tried not to look at the letter. She felt a sudden acidity in her eyes, but she kept fighting the tears. The last thing she needed was to cry in front of her manager.

Mr. Stipp stood behind Patty, looking like her bodyguard, in case Adina decided to make a wrong move.

"This is a copy of your termination letter," said Patty, "which you will also receive in the mail. There is no need for you to stay. You can go now. Do you have any personal belongings for which you need a box?"

Patty smiled as she asked. She was obviously happy to see Adina leave.

It hadn't registered in Adina's mind yet that she was being fired immediately—on the spot. In a cracked voice, she braced herself and asked her manager, "So you mean today is the last day?" Her voice trembled and was barely audible as she fought tears.

"Yes, today, actually now, is your last time here," said Mr. Stipp. "Pack up all your things and make sure you delete any personal emails. Do you have any personal emails?"

Personal emails? Yeah, right! Was this a trap to see whether Adina admitted to using the workplace for personal emails? *Smart, Mr. Stipp!*

"No, I don't have any personal emails," Adina said, hoping this might help Mr. Stipp to change his decision and let her keep her job after all. But she could see in his eyes that there was no way back. She needed to be strong—and to leave before she exploded in pieces in front of them.

"Thank you," Adina said, not knowing why she was thanking them. By then, tears were making their way down her cheeks, causing a fog in her eyes. Patty victoriously left her office, knowing Adina would never press any charges, or make it hard for them to terminate her like some employees, who complained to their unions or even sued their employers. Adina's job level also belonged to the union, and she had been paying a union membership fee deducted out of her bi-weekly pay. But because her employment status was probationary, she didn't have the same rights as those with full-time status, even though she worked full-time hours, and overtime, for which she wasn't allowed to be paid.

Adina wasn't as much hurt by being fired as she was by being humiliated in front of her coworkers. It seemed like everybody had known about her impending termination, except her. Even Sylvia, with whom she shared her office, hadn't said anything to her. But Adina was sure Sylvia knew because she got along well with Patty, who always praised her work. Patty acted as a mentor to Sylvia and had done so since day one of her hiring. Both were graduates from the University of Wisconsin—Patty in Finance, and Sylvia in Marketing. Adina had graduated from the University of Maryland and majored in Business Communications.

Both Sylvia and Adina had been hired at the same time, but while Adina was overwhelmed with work from day one, Sylvia complained about not having enough work. She often played cards on her computer because she was bored without anything to keep her busy. When Sylvia had asked Patty whether she could do some of Adina's work, Patty had told her not to help Adina under any circumstances. Sylvia was clearly underworked, while Adina had on her plate all kinds of reporting issues and deadlines, and was in charge of correcting old reporting errors. Many times, Sylvia had confided in Adina that she was afraid she would be let go because she was underemployed. But now, it was Adina getting fired instead.

After Adina shed some tears, she caught her breath and decided she would leave with her head held high. But the more she tried to be brave, the more the emotions took hold of her.

What if I actually have no talent? She thought to herself as self-doubts crept in. This was terrible; she felt a rush of cold run down her spine, and she started shaking. Adina jumped when Maria entered her office and said, "I'm sorry, kid," and really meant it. She enveloped her with a warm bear hug, which caused Adina to cry even harder. Maria helped Adina quickly pack up her belongings, which consisted of her kids' pictures she had hung on the wall, some silly African figurines, a binder containing some personal notes, and the termination letter she had received from Patty.

As Adina left the office, she saw her trainer peeking at her from her office door, happy to see her leave. Her other coworkers were mostly silent, almost fearing for their own jobs, while a few talked to fill the silence. But for Adina, it was the shame of her life; her worst fear had manifested. In her mind, if she couldn't manipulate Macros and VLOOKUPs in the Excel software, then she had no real talent, and was probably as stupid as Patty had hinted during their one-on-one meetings. Adina had always kept her face straight whenever Patty had launched into her condescending rants.

Adina was intimidated by the Excel software, the way height intimidates acrophobes. Her trainer had noticed Adina's fear and used it against her. She had put her down, screamed at her, and reported her "incompetence" to their manager. It had never occurred to Adina that she could have asked her trainer to stop her bullying behavior. She had never said anything to Patty either. Adina hated confrontation, and she didn't believe in tattling on other employees. Therefore, she had internalized her frustration the entire time she was on the job.

When Adina got home that day, it was earlier than usual. Her kids instantly noticed the sadness on their mother's face. Adina's personality was usually cheerful, so Geneva and Haile knew something was wrong.

"Mom, why are you home so early?" Geneva and Haile asked in unison.

Adina tried to be a good sport, but when she muttered something, she choked on her words.

"Mom, what's wrong?" Geneva asked.

"I've been let go from my job, sweetheart," Adina said, looking like she had been sentenced for life. For a brief moment, the kids didn't grasp what she was saying. They looked at each other for an instant, and then they went to envelop their mother with big hugs while she sobbed on for what seemed like an eternity.

She felt her children's love travel to her very core, a place no one had ever been able to reach in her soul. Their love was so pure, and so unconditional; it made her long for a mother of her own.

"Don't worry, Mom. We'll be fine," Geneva said as if she had a plan.

Haile just sat there, unable to say anything, but visibly upset. He had never seen his mother cry. Adina had always been able to conceal her pain from her children and act cheerful. That's because she did most of her crying in bed at night, when everybody was asleep. And in the mornings, she would feel lighthearted. Shedding tears usually took some of the burden away so she could function normally. But today, she couldn't feel the heavy weight on her heart getting any lighter. She tried to compose herself for her children's sake, but it was more than she could bear.

Adina still had to figure out what she was going to make for dinner that night, but feeling a lack of energy, she decided to order a pizza for delivery. As she was giving her debit card number to the person taking her order on the phone, Adina couldn't help thinking that, soon, without a paycheck, her bank account would be depleted. Except for the small amount of child support her ex-husband Charles paid, she would have no other income, and the child support didn't even cover her apartment rent. Since her divorce, she had managed to make ends meet with temporary work here and there, but this job had promised better pay and benefits after her probation period. That she didn't last even the three months of probation once again proved, in Adina's mind, that she was a total failure.

Although Adina didn't have much savings, she had a little money put away in a ROTH IRA from her small inheritance from her adoptive parents. It wasn't ideal to have to withdraw her savings now, but what other choice did she have? She realized how the mathematical calculation for child support had worked unfavorably for her, and especially to her children's disadvantage. She had long since stopped arguing with her ex-husband about money, just taking the minimum he agreed to pay. She didn't want to spend another penny on lawyers' fees by going to court, so she just took care of everything the kids needed to the best of her ability.

That night, in her bed, Adina tossed and turned. All she could do was think over and over again about how humiliated she felt being fired in front of everybody at work. She closed her eyes and envisioned how the situation could have been handled differently. She wished her employer could have let her finish the work day and then told her not to come back the next day. Or, since the next day was Friday, they could have let her work one more day to finish out the week. That Patty and Mr. Stipp couldn't wait for one more day to fire her was an extra sting to Adina's soul. She felt rejected all over again, like when, as an orphan, she had been mistreated during her early childhood in Ethiopia. She had never sunk so low in her life.

It was about 4 a.m. when Adina finally crashed, exhausted beyond comprehension, and fell asleep. Two hours later, she heard Geneva getting ready for school and woke up with a start. She felt like she had a hangover, even though she hadn't had a drink in months. Her stomach was tied into a knot, and she felt dizzy when she stood up to go to the bathroom, so she sat back quickly on the edge of her bed. Then she heard the door slam; Geneva was leaving for school.

Adina decided to go back to bed, hoping to grab a couple of minutes of sleep before waking her son. But as soon as she closed her eyes, flashes of her being fired the day before came rushing into her mind. She couldn't get this mind of hers to be silent, or still. Now wide awake, she got out of bed and went into the kitchen to make herself a cup of coffee. At least she would be home now when her son left for school and when her kids came home. She lightened up a little at the idea of being home for her children. Maybe raising them was her destiny, her true calling in life. She didn't mind it, except that there were still bills to pay. The thought of bills painted a grim image in Adina's mind, but she refused to let it spoil the benefit of being home for her children.

After the first sip of her coffee, Adina felt a little hope deep down in her heart. Something was telling her things would be okay, but she didn't know how. *Maybe it's the caffeine kicking in, girlfriend!* She teased herself. Or maybe, this was a glimpse of hope, a sign of God letting her know that she and her children were going to be fine. After she sent Haile off to school, her phone rang. It was Bella calling to check on her mother. Geneva had texted her sister that their mother was out of a job and was very depressed about it.

"Mom, what happened, and how are you?" Bella knew this would have an impact on her as well since her mother supplemented her college scholarship, sending her money every now and then.

"I am fine, sweetheart; don't worry about me. How are you?" Adina tried to avoid being too emotional about her situation for her daughter's sake.

She had always encouraged her children to reach for the stars, and never let anything or anyone limit them. She wished she could apply that same wisdom to herself, but it wasn't easy. Bella and her mother talked until Bella had to go to class, but she promised she would call her mother again later. Adina knew she was lucky to have such loving children; it was one blessing she never took for granted. She said a prayer that morning, thanking God, and asking Him to protect her kids.

CHAPTER 2

Once Adina was alone with her thoughts, she began to realize how being fired had reignited some old wounds she had tried to conceal over the years. She suddenly felt the same deep sense of loss and rejection she had experienced when she lost her beloved adoptive parents in a plane crash. They had been the only family Adina had ever known, and her eyes welled up at the memory of how they had given her a hand to hold and a second chance in life, before she even knew what life meant. She had only been a small child when her adoptive parents rescued her from the orphanage in Ethiopia and brought her to America, away from the harsh elements of the orphanage where she had been placed in Addis Ababa. She knew nothing of her or her family's history prior to her adoption when she was five. What little she did know was what her adoptive mother had told her later, after she had been adopted; and even then, she hadn't known the full story.

Adina's biological mother, Abeba, had been a tall, vibrant Ethiopian girl, with the beauty of the Queen of Sheba. At sixteen, she could already turn men's heads. She lived with her maternal uncle, Berhanu Lule, while attending school in Ethiopia's capital, Addis Ababa. Her uncle was a government employee in the Ethiopian ministry of foreign affairs. He had brought his niece Abeba from her native village in northern Ethiopia to give her a chance to attend school. Abeba's widowed mother couldn't afford her daughter's education, so she had asked her brother for help. In Abeba's village, girls were not encouraged to go to school, but her mother wanted a different life for her daughter. She had not been able to attend school because she was a girl; her father had preferred to send her brother Berhanu, only because he was a boy. Instead, Abeba's mother had been married off at fifteen.

Abeba's uncle was a young professional in his thirties. Berhanu worked for "Boss," as he called his boss, the minister of foreign affairs. In his fifties, Boss had a distinguished look and an air of nobility about him and used his position quite often to get what he wanted. Boss was a married man with two sons. He was also Berhanu's good friend, so he liked to visit him regularly at his house, where he lived with his niece Abeba who was in the tenth grade. Abeba looked older than her real age, and men in the city of Addis Ababa never failed to notice her when she passed by on her way to or from school. As Abeba had grown older, Berhanu's boss had increased his visits to their house. One day, Boss asked Berhanu to go to Sudan for a two days' work assignment. Berhanu left on a Thursday night, and Boss assured him that he would look after Abeba while he was gone.

On that Thursday night, Boss came to see Abeba at her uncle's house, where she was helping the houseboy make dinner—some *injera* (bread) and beef stew. Since Berhanu wasn't married yet, Abeba had assumed the female role in the house and made sure everything was organized. That was what her mother had told her to do.

"Be a good girl, Abeba. Don't bring shame on your uncle's life or mine. Work in the house and around the house. Don't sit cross-legged like those city girls I have seen; make yourself useful! Do you understand me?" Her mother had told Abeba this before sending her off to live with her uncle in the big city.

"So, should I just skip school and do the housework?" Abeba had challenged her mother. But her mother had given her one of her looks that said, "Shut up. I don't want to hear another word from you."

"Greetings, Abeba," said Boss when he arrived at her house.

"Hello, sir," said Abeba, stepping aside to let him inside.

"I told your uncle I would check on you while he is away. Is there anything you need, my child?" Boss asked as he sat in the living room.

"No, sir. I have everything I need, but you are welcome to share dinner with us. The houseboy is just finishing up," Abeba shyly replied.

"In that case, I'll make myself comfortable! Why don't you come and sit here in the living room with me? We can chat about your school work and how you're doing. You know, I helped your uncle to secure that enrollment for you! They had asked him to pay a fat bribe for your transfer, but I arranged it myself. The principal is an old friend of mine," Boss said, before adding, "I suppose you owe me then!"

Abeba respectfully complied with his request and took a seat in the living room. Boss was treating himself to a glass of whiskey he had poured for himself—the same Berhanu offered him whenever he visited. He already knew where Berhanu kept liquors for important guests. Shortly after, the houseboy called them into the dining room. At the dinner table, Boss talked animatedly to Abeba who wasn't really listening or talking, but only nodded out of respect.

After dinner, Abeba helped the houseboy clear the table as her uncle's boss retreated to the living room. He seemed to think this was his house; he was making himself too comfortable, which started to anguish Abeba. She wanted the house to herself, so she could call her best friend and chat for hours since her uncle was not home to limit her phone time. Berhanu only allowed her to call her friends after her homework was done.

After tidying up the dining room and the kitchen, the houseboy told Abeba that it was time for him to go home to his wife and kids in the city suburbs. He only came to Berhanu's house during the day and stayed until after dinner; then he went home to his own family.

"Good night, sir. Thank you for keeping Abeba company," the houseboy said to Boss. He had come to like Boss's down-to-earth nature, despite his being high up in the Ethiopian government. The houseboy himself was an older man, even though they called him a houseboy. Most housekeepers were young males, but anyone who could do the job and earn a little money was referred to as a *houseboy*. The man really didn't mind the title; it wasn't like a different one would have changed anything. Houseboys were still at the bottom of society's hierarchy, cooking and cleaning for others to earn a little money. So he was grateful for the job; plus, Berhanu had become like family to him. Berhanu gave him clothes for his older sons—anything he didn't want to wear anymore. And sometimes, if there were any food left, Berhanu told him he could take it to his family. So the houseboy enjoyed these perks, in addition to his salary. He loved Berhanu like a brother, not a master.

"Goodnight!" Boss replied. "You should find me a houseboy who is as clean as you are! I like how tidy you make this house!"

"Yes, sir, I shall find you one and let you know. Goodnight, sir," the houseboy said as he picked up his bag and left.

Boss excused himself to use the bathroom. Abeba had hoped he would leave when the houseboy did, but now she felt chills up her spine; he was clearly planning to stay for a while.

When Boss returned to the living room, Abeba was sitting in the chair farthest from where he had been sitting. He stopped in the doorway for a minute and gave Abeba a creepy look.

"Hahaha, why are you sitting so far away from me child? I don't bite. Come sit near me!" Boss sat down on the sofa and tapped the spot beside him to show Abeba where he wanted her to sit.

"No, it's okay, sir. I'm comfortable here," she replied.

"Oh, okay. Maybe then I should be the one moving closer to you!"

He stood up from his chair and sat down on the floor in front of Abeba. His back was facing Abeba's knees. He reached up to touch her hand, and then he started caressing her thighs.

"You know, at your age, Abeba," he said, "girls are tender and ripe like the red tomatoes in your uncle's little garden. There is no need to wait when a fruit is ripe; you just have to harvest it."

At that moment, his hand slid up her thigh again, but this time, he dipped his hand into Abeba's underwear.

Abeba's body instantly froze. She started to stand up and move from where she was sitting, but Boss was stronger and more robust. He took her in his arms as she struggled to run. He pressed her down on the tiled floor, and he raped her right there in the living room, in her uncle's house. As he penetrated her, Abeba lost her bearings—and her consciousness. She woke up after what seemed to have been two hours from a nightmare she couldn't completely remember, nor forget, to the sight of blood on her underwear.

In the meantime, Boss had left. He had gone home to his wife, who never suspected her husband was a rapist.

Abeba never recovered from the rape. She became ill almost immediately, throwing up every day. When her uncle returned home, he didn't know what was wrong with her. At first, he suspected it could be a bad menstrual cycle, but when it continued for a few days, he knew it had to be more than that—he just didn't know what. He asked Abeba, but, of course, she couldn't tell her uncle what had happened with his boss in his absence—on the tiled floor in his living room. Berhanu was a man of morals. He would not have believed that his boss could have done such a thing. She knew he would probably kill her before she could kill herself, so she kept silent. He couldn't have faced such shame brought on him by his niece. Plus, Abeba knew no one, male or female, would ever believe her. In her culture, rape was believed to be the girl's fault; no one else was to blame.

When Abeba's vomiting didn't subside after two weeks, her uncle took her to the dispensary near his office and told her he would return to pick her up after work. The nurse on duty, who performed the checkup on Abeba, noticed some bruising on her thighs and asked her about it.

Abeba only burst into tears and refused to tell the nurse what had happened. But the nurse automatically knew; she just didn't know who had done it, but she intended to find out.

"Who did this to you, Abeba?" the nurse repeated, but Abeba only cried and shook her head, refusing to tell her.

In her twenty-year nursing career, the nurse had seen other girls come to the dispensary for treatment after being raped, so this wasn't new to her. While some girls were raped by strangers, more often than not, the crime was committed by relatives or people who were close to the victim.

So the nurse asked Abeba bluntly, "Was this done by your uncle?"

"No, no. And stop asking me. Stop insulting my uncle!" Abeba was now screaming at the nurse and crying openly.

The nurse just hugged Abeba and gave her a shoulder to cry on, which was wet after their embrace. Abeba felt a little better then as she blew her nose and sat up straight on the examining bed. Finally, she found her courage and told the nurse what had happened, and how she didn't remember all the details because she lost consciousness during the act.

"That rat, that rotten rat!" the nurse said. Like Abeba, she knew girls were not allowed to bring forth these cases for justice. Women just kept such crimes a secret, while the rapists walked free. To avoid being shunned by society, raped women and girls told no one what had happened to them—not even their parents or closest friends. It seemed as if society worked together with the rapist so he could freely commit his crime and go unpunished.

Three months later, Abeba started feeling better. But she also started gaining a little weight. She was a thin girl to begin with, more tall than big. But her clothes started to fit too tightly, especially around her waistline. The nurse from the dispensary started visiting Abeba at her uncle's house. She also told Abeba to tell her uncle what had happened with Boss, but Abeba vehemently refused. She didn't need to get her uncle fired if he chose to confront his boss. Now past her initial fear, she began to think her uncle might take her side and fight his boss on her behalf. That's how much she knew Berhanu loved her.

One day, the nurse came to visit Abeba while her uncle was still at work. She noticed Abeba's waistline looked bigger, and as she observed her, Abeba's belly moved. The nurse approached her and touched her belly, and she felt it again!

"Abeba, my child, you're pregnant!" the nurse announced.

Abeba's soul had almost left her body when the rape happened. Why would God now punish her in this way? She hadn't done anything wrong; she had been assaulted by her uncle's boss, and now she carried that man's child? Abeba started to scream, and it tore at the nurse's heart. Abeba cried, shaking all the while as she gripped the nurse's shoulder.

"Please help me abort it before my uncle finds out! Please!" Abeba pleaded with the nurse.

"No, child, I will not do such a thing. A baby is a gift from God, no matter how it is made," the nurse replied. "Plus, it's too late now anyway, and too risky."

Abeba thought she would rather die than carry this baby. She didn't know how she could get it out of her womb, and the nurse refused to help her abort it. Abeba thought she might just kill herself since there was no other way out. At least that way, her uncle and mother wouldn't have to face the shame of her bringing a "bastard" into the world. It would be a disgrace to her family, and she had heard horrific stories of young girls ostracized, and even killed, by their own families because they wanted to avoid being shunned by the community.

In her culture, if a girl got pregnant out of wedlock, her family suffered as well. In some cases, the whole family was stripped of all their property and possessions and kicked off their land. Abeba knew that's what would happen to her mother, who didn't have much to begin with. The small land her mother owned would be taken away, and she would be kicked out of her thatched hut. Abeba could see that there was no other way out—dying was her only solution. But each day, she struggled to find the courage to take her own life.

Abeba was at the end of her pregnancy's first trimester when her school principal telephoned her uncle.

"Hello, Mr. Lule? Yes, Principal Tesfaye here. I want to inform you that the school has decided to expel Abeba. It's quite unfortunate because we thought she would have a bright future, but it's against school policy to have pregnant girls in school."

Until then, Abeba's uncle had never suspected anything. He had assumed Abeba was experiencing bad growing pains and menstruations that would eventually fade away as she grew mature.

As soon as her uncle learned about her pregnancy, he rebuked Abeba and sent her back to the village to her mother.

"Don't you ever come back here! You are a disgrace! You've brought shame and dishonor to my entire family!" Berhanu exclaimed as he threw her clothes and other belongings out the door. "Go now! Get out of here, and never come back. Gooo…!"

Once back in her village, Abeba had to face her community's wrath. By her second trimester, her dress was too tight on her belly so her pregnancy was obvious. She carried the pregnancy with all the disgrace that came with having a child out of wedlock. At eight-and-a-half months, Abeba couldn't carry the pregnancy to term. The baby in her womb was getting too big, and her frame was too small to carry it any longer. With the help of midwives in her mother's village, Abeba gave birth to a premature, but beautiful baby girl. Unfortunately, she didn't survive the ordeal of childbirth and died an hour after the baby was born.

Abeba's mother was left with no other choice than to take care of her daughter's baby, despite the shame that accompanied it. She nurtured the infant until no one could believe she was a premature baby. Abeba's mother gave her grandbaby the love and care needed to offset the wrath and humiliation her daughter had gone through.

Her grandmother named her grandbaby Adina, which in Amharic means "She has saved." When Adina turned two, Abeba's mother died, leaving her in the care of a distant cousin and his wife who had nine children of their own.

Meanwhile, Berhanu was no longer living in Addis Ababa. He had received a good position at the World Bank and moved to the United States of America, where he had married. He and his wife lived in Bethesda, Maryland, and they had eventually started a family.

Since kicking Abeba out of his house, Berhanu had never asked about her. He didn't want to associate with someone who had brought shame on his family, and he no longer visited his sister, Abeba's mother, before her death.

In the care of her distant relatives, Adina was mistreated. Her second cousin's wife didn't appreciate that her husband had brought another child into the home when they already had nine of their own children to provide for. Many times, she fed her own children, but didn't give any food to Adina, who sometimes resorted to eating what had been dropped on the floor by the other kids. If Adina made a mistake, she was severely punished more than the other children. One day, Adina's second cousin learned that the Ethiopian government had started allowing orphans to be adopted overseas, and so, he took Adina to the orphanage in Addis Ababa. She was three years old.

CHAPTER 3

In America, two lovebirds, Mitch Springfield and Shelly Thompson met in medical school at Columbia University. Shelly was from Australia and had come to the United States as an international student, but had ended up staying. Mitch was a native of New Hampshire. He had just finished his undergraduate studies at the University of New England, and came to Columbia to attend the obstetric program. Shelly was a professor's assistant, in the Department of Health Administration, trying to make a little money to finish her Doctorate in Health Administration. One morning, Shelly and Mitch met for the first time in the cafeteria—and they fell in love almost instantly. Shelly was rushing to her class, so she promised to meet up with him after her classes that evening. Mitch took her to an Irish pub not far from their university campus, where they stayed and talked until the wee hours.

On their sixth-month dating anniversary, Mitch proposed to Shelly and she accepted. They decided to move in together in Shelly's apartment. Her job at the university allowed her to rent her own fully furnished apartment, and it was more than large enough to accommodate them both. In addition, it was located in the university's vicinity, within walking distance, since Shelly didn't have a car.

For Mitch, this was it—he had found the girl he wanted to marry, and he called and told his parents that night that he was engaged. His parents sounded surprised, but they knew better than to interfere in Mitch's life. He was his own man now, allowed to make his own choices in life, and experience the consequences or reap the rewards that came with those choices. But when they heard his enthusiasm on the phone, they thought maybe he had found the right girl. They decided to invite him and Shelly for Thanksgiving dinner in New Hampshire, and once they met her, they were very pleased with their future daughter-in-law.

Six years of marriage passed, but during that time, Shelly and Mitch had no children. Shelly was approaching the big forty, so her chances of getting pregnant were becoming slim, if not null. She had undergone a series of fertility treatments and gotten pregnant numerous times, but she couldn't carry the pregnancy even to the first term. The doctors found she had a rare condition that prevented her from carrying a baby in her uterus. Both Shelly and her husband worked hard at their respective careers, she as a Health Administrator, and he as an OB/GYN at Boston General Hospital. They loved what they did, but it made Mitch sad that he could help women deliver babies, but he couldn't make his own child. After her last attempt of in-vitro failed, Shelly told her husband she wanted to adopt.

"Honey, we've tried everything! I'm just not meant to be a biological mother," Shelly had told her husband several times after each failed pregnancy.

Mitch wanted to have his own kids, but after all the miscarriages, he agreed that the only option left was to adopt. They looked in many countries, and they worked with different adoption agencies, but they never had a chance to be accepted to adopt. They had even gone to Guatemala in hopes of finding a baby to adopt, but they soon found that the political system there made it too complicated.

Back in Ethiopia, the orphanage where Adina lived was chosen to be placed under the international adoption policy. Drs. Shelly and Mitch Springfield had just returned from Guatemala when they heard about it. When they applied to volunteer with the organization Doctors Without Borders, they were sent to Ethiopia on a mission to treat patients who suffered from obstetric *fistula*, a condition many young women in Ethiopia were dying from, better known as childbirth injury. Due to the lack of better surgery equipment, and other needed treatments of infections, many women, especially young mothers died from childbirth more than from any other cause. It was how Adina's mother, Abeba, had died.

In Ethiopia, Shelly and Mitch met the head of the orphanage, and after a great deal of adoption paperwork, they adopted Adina when she was five years old and brought her to America. In their care, Adina blossomed. She developed well and became the joy of Shelly and Mitch Springfield. After their trip from Ethiopia, they decided to move to Bethesda, Maryland, where Mitch started working in obstetrics research at the University of Maryland and Shelly became a hospital administrator at the Children's Hospital.

By the time Adina was ready to attend college, Shelly and Mitch had been working in the medical field for so many years that they decided to open a private obstetric practice in Bethesda. They invested all their savings, in addition to the huge mortgage they took out on their home to build the premises. They also took out other loans to buy all the medical equipment they needed. Their practice was built to be the biggest in Maryland. They planned to have other doctors in the field of reproduction join the practice as partners. There was going to be a fertility treatment department, as well as other departments in reproductive and maternal health, and a wing dedicated for pre-natal care.

However, Fate had other plans. Two days before their grand opening, Dr. Shelly Springfield and her husband died in a plane crash, while returning from a conference in California. They were in a small private jet that belonged to one of their friends. The pilot had lost control in a turbulent zone, and a mechanical failure had caused the plane to crash, killing all the plane's occupants, including the crew.

At that time, Adina was a college sophomore at the University of Maryland. Once again, her world was turned upside down. She was devastated; the parents she had known and loved were now gone in the blink of an eye. It just couldn't be possible. Adina refused to eat in the days following the death of her parents. Her friends were concerned and her best friend, Alice Leah, took her to stay with her family for a couple of months, which helped Adina to recover a little bit. But she had to resume school, and after three months, she did. She had no other choice, especially now that she was an orphan for the second time. Because her parents had poured everything they owned into the new medical center, which the banks then foreclosed on, Adina was left penniless and knew she would have to finish school and find a career to support herself.

In her heart of hearts, Adina believed there had to be a purpose for all this to happen to her. When she thought about where she had come from, she knew the hand of God had shielded her when she had been placed for adoption from a country devastated by famine, diseases, and other problems. Adina always prayed at night, as her adoptive mother had taught her. Now those who had given her that life were gone. At the same time, she was thankful for the blessings they had given her. They had brought her up with love and grace, taught her always to help those who were suffering, and to be a person of integrity, no matter her own circumstances.

"Sometimes your suffering is a gift because it allows you to empathize with other people's pain, and help them," Shelly had told Adina whenever she came home with a heavy heart after having a tough day.

"If I had had children of my own, I probably wouldn't have met you, sweetheart, or helped the other children and their mothers in Ethiopia!" Shelly would tell Adina, adding, "Always see your own sufferings as a step in your journey, and know that they won't last. Everything in life changes—the good as well as the bad. But it's how you perceive it, and how you respond to your adversities that will make or break you." When Adina was ten, Shelly had shared with her the story of her adoption, with the information she had been told by the orphanage staff. It wasn't the whole story, just that her mother Abeba was a sixteen-year-old high school student when she had her. Shelly also told Adina that her biological mother had died right after giving birth to her, from a condition called *fistula*. However, there was no information regarding whom her biological father had been.

Shelly always inspired her daughter to see the good even in the ugliness of life. Shelly's own mother had died when Shelly was a teenager, so she empathized with Adina on a deeper level. She and Mitch were a match made in heaven, and Adina was amazed by how much they loved each other and her. She only hoped she could be so lucky in life as to meet and marry a good man, like her adoptive mother had. Mitch was kind-hearted, mischievous, and full of life. It was hard for Adina to believe her parents were now gone, and so tragically.

Adina reflected on what her adoptive mother used to tell her. "You must follow your heart, even if it means some setbacks. Always listen to that little faint inner voice. That's God talking to you!" Shelly would say.

After Adina returned to the University of Maryland, she wasn't herself anymore. She felt as if something in her soul had been taken away. She wasn't focused on her studies, and her grades suffered. But she had to keep up and graduate on time, especially now that she was all alone again. She would need the degree to find a job to provide for herself. She was very pensive and reflective. As she thought about all her adoptive mother used to teach her about life, tears welled up and filled her eyes. Her heart was filled with too much sorrow. She had lost the only parents known to her. But she had to go on, and learn how to live alone again in this world.

CHAPTER 4

The afternoon after she had been let go from work, Adina called her best friend, Alice Leah, whom her friends called Aleah for short.

"Hi, Sista! *Whazup?*" Aleah answered, laughing out loud, because she had recognized Adina's name on the caller I.D. For a moment, Adina was silent, not echoing her friend's enthusiasm.

"Adina? Hello!" said Aleah, but all she heard was Adina blowing her nose and sniffling.

"Adina, honey, what's wrong? Talk to me. Are you okay? Are the kids all right?" Aleah asked, now worried, and all her usual teasing went out the door. She could feel something was wrong in her friend's silence. She knew Adina too well, even better than Adina knew herself.

"Yes…. No…. I mean I'm fine, and the kids are all right," Adina answered in a whisper.

"So, what's up with all that sniffling? Please tell me quickly; I'm going crazy here assuming the worst."

Knowing she had to let out her grief and that Aleah was like the sister she never had, Adina poured forth her story.

"It's just…I lost my job. They fired me, Aleah! You know how much I needed that job. Now I'm unemployed. And worst of all, they fired me in front of everybody, yesterday at 3 p.m.! They couldn't even give me one more day to finish out the week," Adina said, as she choked on her words and tears flowed down her face.

"The bastards! I'm coming, Adina; I'm getting on the bus tomorrow morning to see you, and don't bother saying it's not necessary. I will not listen to your nonsense. I'm taking the first bus from D.C."

"I'm fine, Aleah, really; you don't have to come."

"The hell I don't have to come! Of course I don't have to, but I want to. You sound like a mess, Adina. I will be there tomorrow, end of discussion!" Aleah confirmed authoritatively.

Adina knew there was no point arguing with her best friend once her mind was made up. They talked some more about her ended job, then their kids and some other subjects, and Aleah started again the conversation Adina didn't want to have.

"You need to talk to your damn ass of an ex, Adina!" said Aleah, who had never liked Charles Kumi.

"What for, Aleah? To tell him I've been fired? I don't want to hear his sarcasm," Adina replied. Talking to

Charles was the last thing Adina wanted to do. He had a way of bringing out the worst in her, so she didn't want to tell him about her failures. He had been glad when she never claimed more child support, and they had each settled into their own lives.

"Adina, listen to me. Charles needs to give you more money for the kids now that you don't have a job. Why do you let him get away with everything? He has a good job, and that came from your sacrificing for his career while you took the backseat. Don't you think you deserve his support?" Aleah continued.

"Aleah, you know better than anyone that Charles doesn't care about the children, or me. All he cares about is himself, and I have accepted who he is. I can't change him; God knows I tried for eighteen years!" Adina began to sound even more depressed; she really hated having to talk to her ex-husband.

"Honey, please, I'm begging you. You can't carry the burden of child-rearing alone when the kids still have a father. At least promise me you'll try. You owe that to your children, Adina!"

Aleah was insistent, and she made a lot of sense—Adina knew it. Why did she have to forgo financial support for her children? She could take Charles to court if he refused to cooperate. She knew talking to him would mean another war between them, but she promised Aleah to give it a try.

After they hung up, Adina felt much better than she had since being terminated. Her friend always helped alleviate some of the pain by helping her talk it out. Adina tended to keep everything inside, but Aleah was the exact opposite. She was outspoken and never took any nonsense from anyone. Unlike Aleah, Adina hated confrontation and conflicts; she talked with a smooth voice and was gentle, quiet, and reserved. She confided in no one, except Aleah.

As Adina made dinner that night, she thought a lot about Aleah, and how she seemed to have it all together in her life. She enjoyed her marriage to James Mushoi, a fellow from Kenya, who was a professor of African History at Howard University. Aleah worked in the Maryland public school district's administration, overseeing high school curriculum, and she was passionate about her career. Her twin sons were blossoming in college at Howard, tuition-free, since their father worked there. Aleah never had any trouble fitting into the community where she lived, unlike Adina. Adina had always felt like an outsider wherever she had lived since she had come to America. She looked different from her white adoptive parents, most of her classmates, and everyone else in her surroundings. Since kindergarten, she had endured her classmates calling her names like "Chocolate Milk" and asking her whether her mother drank too much coffee when she was pregnant with her. Adina had always been irked by how she couldn't fit in, but she had grown used to it. She knew some of her classmates' questions and teasing were due to their not being exposed to a wider society or culture beyond their communities. Some kids had never seen a black person up close and personal before her. Nonetheless, it had saddened Adina not to look or be like the other kids. No matter what her adoptive parents tried to put her at ease, Adina could never feel that she belonged. But she had accepted it.

Aleah was never afraid to express her opinions, and she never let anyone bully her. She loved to quote Eleanor Roosevelt: "No one can make you feel inferior without your consent." Adina wished she could adhere to Mrs. Roosevelt's wisdom. In retrospect, Adina thought that what Aleah had always told her about letting her ex-husband walk all over her and get away with everything was true in a way. That night, she decided she would go talk to Charles and ask him for more financial support for the kids.

Adina was grateful to have Aleah as a friend she could trust. When Aleah had seen Adina for the first time, it was during lunch recess on the first day of school at Walt Whitman High School when Aleah had just transferred to the school. She quickly noticed Adina and how beautiful she was. They seemed to be the only black people in the school cafeteria. Aleah approached the table where Adina was sitting.

"Can I sit here?" Aleah asked, but not really—it was more of an announcement because it wasn't like the students at the table would have said that she couldn't. And if they had dared, they would have known who the true Aleah was. She didn't bully anyone, but neither did anyone bully her. She exuded the kind of self-confidence that could be confused with too much pride, and even inspired fear at times. If anyone had the misfortune of crossing her, Aleah could be a bit aggressive. She liked to say that the streets of Baltimore, where she grew up, had prepped her for the real world.

"Of course!" Adina replied as Aleah sat down at her table. Her shy smile instantly put Aleah at ease.

"Girl, these white kids are so loud; I can't even hear myself think!" Aleah told Adina under her breath so the white kids at the table wouldn't hear her.

Adina laughed out loud this time, because if anyone was being loud, it was Aleah. Adina envied her ease at a new school. After they finished their sandwiches, Adina split her dark chocolate candy bar in two, and handed one half to Aleah.

"Girl, what's this?" Aleah asked with a disgusted face.

"Chocolate, dark chocolate. It's supposed to be good for you," Adina said as she munched on her half.

"And you believe in that bullshit? Girl, I want a real chocolate donut, with a pound of caramel on it. Not this sour, dark, disgusting, thing! Are you trying to lose weight or something? Oh! Wait, are you trying to say that I need to lose weight?" Aleah asked as she snapped her fingers with an attitude.

Surely, this girl didn't hold back. Adina laughed and thought she could use a friend with a sense of humor—and an attitude to boot. Aleah had nothing to worry about in the weight department, of course. Her mother was a nutritionist, she made sure Aleah only ate healthy food, which was why sometimes Aleah craved calories and sugar. But she was well-built at seventeen years old and 5'7" tall; she had strong bones, and some muscles, compared to Adina who was taller, but a bit too bony.

From that day on, Adina and Aleah became inseparable best friends. When they graduated, they both attended the University of Maryland. After college graduation, they had gone their separate ways, but remained best friends. They attended each other's milestone events: weddings, children's births, baptisms, birthdays, and kids' graduations. They were there for each other during life's storms, heartaches, trials and tribulations, and they had never once had a fallout in their friendship.

Being both only children, they had come to be like sisters to one another; and in that regard, they were even closer than biological siblings. Theirs was a strong bond that only identical twins could share.

CHAPTER 5

Charles Kumi was a United Nations employee working in the department of Statistics, in New York City. He and Adina had divorced after eighteen years of marriage. He was still single, after two years of being divorced, but he had a long history of womanizing, well-known by most of the UN women in his department. Charles mostly went after the young women who wore tight dresses that showed off their "assets," as he called their big butts.

Charles's parents lived in Southfield, Michigan, where they led a small non-denominational church frequented mostly by the West African community of immigrants. His father was a first generation West African immigrant, who had come from Ghana in the 1960s, following Ghana's independence in 1957. He had been one of the scholars who studied abroad, and had attended a Christian College in Michigan and became a reverend. He ministered to his non-denominational church congregation, while Charles's mother was a homemaker. Charles was the youngest of four children, and his mother was close to fifty when she had him—a miracle baby as she loved to say.

Charles grew up in a preacher's house, with rigorous house rules. But when he became a teenager, he started rebelling against his father's tight rules and the many restrictions put on him. Charles couldn't go out like other teenage boys in his neighborhood, so he had no social life until he went away to college at Virginia State University. While in college, he became a hard partier and learned how to smooth-talk girls into liking him. Despite not liking to go to church, Charles occasionally attended the Episcopal Church in Richmond, with the sole purpose of meeting "nice, well-behaved girls," as he put it.

"I will marry a nice, beautiful, virgin girl as soon as I get out of here," he liked to tell his friends in college.

It was there, at the Episcopal Church, that he had spotted Adina one Easter Sunday. Adina always came to church to pray for her dead adoptive parents. It was her way of feeling close to them as she asked God to let them rest in peace.

After church that Easter Sunday, Charles had approached Adina.

"Hi, I'm Charles. Happy Easter!" Charles introduced himself.

"Adina. Nice to meet you. Happy Easter too," Adina replied, noticing what handsome, dark-glowing skin he had and that he was tall, towering over her by a couple of inches.

"Do you come to this church very often?" Charles asked, not missing her deep beautiful dimples when she smiled.

"Yes, this is my church; I come here every Sunday when I'm not working," Adina answered.

"Really, you work? A beautiful girl like you should not work!" Charles said. It was his favorite pick-up line for every girl he was interested in sleeping with, but of course, Adina didn't know that.

"Well, some of us need to work," Adina replied with a shy smile, trying to conceal how attracted to him she felt.

They sat on a bench in the back of the church, and talked for two straight hours. It was 2 p.m. when Adina realized she was going to be late for work if she didn't run. She left for her work afternoon shift at the Ethiopian restaurant where she had found a part-time job. It was her senior year in college, and she couldn't wait to finish school, and find a real job where she could use her business communications major.

Both Charles and Adina were finishing school that spring, him at Virginia State University, and Adina at the University of Maryland. Adina surprised herself by how she opened up to Charles so quickly. She had promised herself that she would never date anyone until she graduated. But it seemed like she was breaking her own self-imposed rules.

The following Sunday, Charles showed up at church, hoping to meet Adina again. This time, he had decided he would ask her out, and he was sure she would say yes. During the service, he looked everywhere in the chapel, but he didn't see her. Whatever the preacher said that Sunday was just background noise. Charles's mind was busy wondering where the hell Adina was. She had given him her cell phone number, and told him which campus apartments she lived in at University of Maryland. When Charles noticed she wasn't in the church, he left before the end of the service and went to look for her at her campus apartment. He knocked on the door twice before Adina opened it. She was in her pajamas when she opened the door. Her roommate was gone for the weekend to visit her boyfriend out of town.

"I thought you said you never miss church," Charles said, repeating what she had told him when they had met on Easter.

"True, unless I have to work late, which is what I did last night," Adina replied.

"So, you work at night too?" Charles asked.

"Yep, and last night was very busy; because we hosted a wedding reception till the wee hours. I came home at

3 a.m., thus missing church this morning. But I'll go to the evening service," Adina said. "Hold on a minute and I'll get dressed." She went into the other room to change out of her pajamas, and put on her jogging pants and a T-shirt.

"Have you eaten breakfast yet?" Charles called to her while she was changing. "I'm starving! Can you make me some eggs?" It sounded more like an order than a request, but Adina didn't mind.

"Make you eggs? Okay, sure!" she said, returning to the kitchen. She opened the small cabinet where she kept her pans and started cooking two omelets. Then they sat down on the couch and ate the omelet, toasted bread, and coffee. They talked about many things, including their childhoods, and Adina surprised herself by opening up to Charles about her origins and how she had never met her biological parents, because they were dead. She shared with him what she knew about her biological mother from what her adoptive parents had told her, which they had learned from the orphanage staff. But Adina never knew who her biological father was, or whether he was dead or still alive. She just assumed he was dead. Then Charles told her about his upbringing in the Detroit metro area, and how he hated his father for not letting him experience anything in his youth.

"Not even television was allowed in my house; forget about video games, or anything else for that matter that didn't revolve around his church. We lived like an Amish family, even though we were less than twenty miles from downtown Detroit," Charles complained.

In the four years he had been at Virginia State University, Charles had only been home for the holidays twice, at his mother's pleading. Charles spent most of the holidays at his friends' houses; he said his friends had cool parents, unlike his. The rest of the time, he just stayed on campus, going around town and partying in nightclubs in Washington, D.C.

"Maybe your dad wanted to protect you from Detroit's mean streets, and that's why he didn't let you get out," Adina reasoned with Charles. She wished he could have enjoyed his childhood since he had his biological parents, and they were still alive. Why was he so angry at his dad, instead of enjoying him before it was too late? You could never know how long you would have your parents. So to Adina, being angry because you didn't get to smoke dope, or drink alcohol, or watch TV as a teenager sounded silly and spoiled. But it mattered to Charles—that was his experience. It didn't mean anything to Adina, but it meant a great deal to him.

"Home was like putting me in jail. That's what it felt like, jail!" Charles said, almost shouting. Talking about his childhood brought out some raw emotions, so Adina resolved not to bring it up again. She didn't say anything more about the subject; she could see that Charles had some unfinished business with his father. A minute later, Charles surprised her by kissing her deep on the mouth, and she responded. And before they could stop the impulse, they were passionately making love and Charles had forgotten all about his father issues. He seemed quite knowledgeable in the sex department, unlike Adina, who was having sex for the very first time. When they came up for air, Adina started to panic.

"Oh my God, what have I done?" She was afraid she might get pregnant just like her sixteen-year-old mother had, a continent away. She prayed hard that night, and she couldn't wait for her next period to come. From now on, she told Charles, they would not have sex again unless they were married. She didn't want to repeat her mother's curse of getting pregnant out of wedlock. But then, Charles introduced her to the world of condoms and they were hooked. They became boyfriend and girlfriend and went steady.

When Adina graduated, both Charles and Aleah came. Adina was excited to introduce her best friend to Charles. She had talked about him so much in the last couple of weeks that she and Charles had been seeing each other. But Aleah took an instant dislike to Charles. She thought he was a bit too cocky from the way he talked about himself. She also noticed that he stared at every girl he saw during their conversation, and she warned Adina about that later at her graduation party.

The following week was Charles's graduation at VSU. His parents came to his graduation, and, of course, Adina went. Charles greeted his parents as if they were distant relatives, and he didn't introduce them to Adina. Adina thought he would get over being upset now that he had graduated and could enter the workforce. She certainly hoped he would because if they were going to be in a long-term relationship, Adina couldn't avoid Charles's parents like he did. In-laws were part of the deal, and she actually wanted to meet and get to know them.

For Adina, having parents was a blessing. She wished she still had hers, but they were gone forever. If she married Charles, then her parents-in-law would be like a new mother and father to her, and she knew she would cherish having them in her life. Charles didn't appreciate what he had, but she continued to encourage him to talk to his dad and clear the air. Since Charles's father didn't initiate the conversation either, Adina knew that reconciling the two of them would not be easy, but she also knew it would be hard for her not to talk to her in-laws.

Charles graduated cum laude with a major in Statistics, and a minor in Data Management. No doubt, he was smart, and in his own words, "a nerd in his spare time." He was offered jobs at the International Monetary Fund, where he had interned, and at the World Bank, but he chose to work for the United Nations in New York City. He said it was about time he lived in a real city, "a city that never sleeps."

Adina continued to work at the Ethiopian restaurant in Virginia, and after her graduation, the owner gave her more hours, but she was looking for a better job in business communications. She sent out a lot of resumes, but it seemed organizations were not inclined to hire her with only waitressing experience. Meanwhile, she and Charles continued to date. He would drive to Virginia where Adina had moved after she finished college, and spent more weekends coming to see her than he stayed in New York City.

"You should move to New York City so I don't have to come here every Friday, Adina," Charles told her when he came for the long Labor Day weekend. "It's a big waste of my hard-earned New York money, you know!"

"You said you come for refills; are you complaining about that too?" Adina teased him after they had just made love.

"Heck no! I'm just saying it would be easier for me if we both lived in New York. And it's not like you have anything keeping you here."

What Charles said made sense. Adina's job at the restaurant wasn't enough reason to keep her in Virginia. And Charles was her first boyfriend and first love, so she didn't want to lose him. But she also loved Berhanu, the restaurant owner, and his wife. They had been good to her over the years. It was the only Ethiopian family she had befriended. Since Berhanu, his wife, and Adina were all Ethiopian-born and living in another country, that was enough for them to feel like they were family. And their three teenage children treated Adina like an older sister, often coming to her for advice about school and dating. Berhanu's wife frequently invited her for home-cooked meals, and she even taught Adina a few words in Amharic since Adina had forgotten her native language, after she came to live with her adoptive parents in America.

When Adina had first come to the restaurant to apply for a job, she had only said her parents had been Ethiopians, but they were dead. She didn't give many more details about her past because she hated talking about her early childhood and only had dim memories of the orphanage. Berhanu had taken an instant liking to the girl and given her a job to help her out with college fees. He also praised her efforts and always encouraged her to stay in school and graduate. Neither suspected the deeper reasons for why they felt connected to one another.

CHAPTER 6

Adina thought about Charles's proposition to move to New York City, and finally agreed. That fall, she moved right into Charles's apartment on Roosevelt Island and never looked back. They got married soon after without too much fanfare. Adina invited a few friends, and so did Charles, but he did not invite his parents. Aleah was Adina's matron of honor, and Aleah's husband and her parents were also there. Adina had also invited Berhanu and his family since he was like the Ethiopian father Adina never had.

On Adina's wedding day, Berhanu walked her down the aisle in the small church on Roosevelt Island, and presented her to Charles. Adina was in love with Charles, but something deep inside her made her question whether she was making a mistake. She felt like she was rushing into marrying him, but she dismissed the feelings as pre-wedding jitters. She knew many brides and even grooms had those doubts right before the wedding. But she also kept thinking about what Aleah had told her when she announced to her best friend that she and Charles were getting married.

"Honey, you should find a good job and establish your career before marrying this dude. A guy who hates his dad because he didn't let him drink or do other crazy stuff is not marriage material." Aleah had repeated similar warnings to Adina over and over again when she helped her find a wedding dress.

But Adina was an orphan and alone in the world. She wanted a family of her own to care for and cherish. Although Berhanu and Aleah's families were good to her, that wasn't enough to quench her thirst for her own family.

When Adina had refused to take her advice, Aleah had finally relinquished her stance and said, "All right! I give up. If Charles makes you happy, then I'm happy for you as well."

Aleah and her parents went out of their way to plan a beautiful small wedding for Adina. She was more than grateful for her friends, who had become her family. Berhanu provided the food and Aleah's parents paid for everything else. Both families considered Adina the second daughter they had never had.

A year after their wedding, Adina and Charles welcomed Bella, their first baby girl. Three years later, Geneva was born. Since Charles was well-established in his career at the UN, Adina decided to stay home to take care of the babies. That's when Charles's behavior worsened. He began having numerous affairs, some of which Adina knew about, and some she didn't. He started telling Adina that she was good for nothing, except having his babies. He went out with some bimbos and would come home drunk and smelling of cheap perfume.

Whenever Adina voiced her concerns about his philandering and drinking too much, Charles would say, "Now you're starting to sound like my father, and you know that's not a compliment because I hate the man!"

By the time Haile was born, Charles was not only a philandering husband; he was also an absentee father. He claimed his work was too demanding for him to spend time at home with the children. He would go on business trips overseas and never call Adina. By then, their marriage was holding on by a thin thread, but Adina had vowed to stay, because divorce was not an option for her. Her family meant everything to her, and no matter how badly Charles behaved, she never wanted a divorce.

They had been married for nearly eighteen years when one night Charles came home drunk. It was past 2 a.m. when he let himself in the bedroom. Without prelude, he pulled the blankets off the bed where Adina was sound asleep and threw them on the floor. Adina felt an instant cold rush and woke up with a start. She quickly sat up on the bed, and the next thing she knew, he had punched her, right there and then. It took her a few seconds to understand what had happened, and then she quickly jumped out of bed and ran out of the bedroom.

"I will kill you if you come back to this room; do you hear me?" Charles shouted. "This is my house, my apartment; that's right! Have you paid any penny on this apartment? Have you? You just move in and expect me to take care of you for only having my babies? Do you think that entitles you to my money?"

Charles cussed her out endlessly, thinking Adina was listening. But she had quickly slipped out of the house and gone next door to her neighbor, Coach Barry, who let her use his phone to call the police. In less than thirty minutes, the police were there, and they took Charles to the station for interrogation. When he came back home the next morning, he looked sober. He packed up his belongings and left. With the help of her friends, Adina filed for divorce. She took the minimum amount Charles agreed to pay for child support, and they parted their ways. To punish Adina further, Charles never adhered to the visitation schedule stipulated in the divorce agreement to see the kids. He wanted Adina to suffer the consequences of calling the police on him and filing for divorce.

After the divorce, Adina began doing temporary work. She had been happy when she finally found a full-time job. Unfortunately, now that she had been fired from it, she was back to square one and had no choice but to ask Charles for more money for the children.

CHAPTER 7

A week after being fired from her job, Adina took the Roosevelt Island Tram to Manhattan, and went to the United Nations Headquarters to meet her ex-husband. Charles didn't like discussing any subject with Adina on the phone; he always dismissed her calls, claiming he was busy in meetings. Adina, therefore, had decided she would have a one-on-one discussion with him in his office. She would surprise him, and she didn't think he'd make a scene and throw her out in front of all the other employees. With that in mind, Adina targeted the noon hour because she knew many UN employees took their lunch breaks then, and she would be best likely to catch him when he wasn't in a meeting.

Adina went to the UN with considerable anxiety and trepidation. She didn't have the patience to listen to Charles's narcissistic speech about her failed career, and how dependent on him she was. Charles always knew what parts of his ex-wife to trigger, what buttons to push and bring out the worst in her. "For my kids' sake, I will meet him." Adina said under her breath, already feeling tense. She decided she would endure his abuse this one last time. At least, she hoped it would be the last.

When she arrived at Charles's office at the UN, the receptionist greeted her, not knowing who she was. Adina gave her name and waited while the receptionist called his office. Until this moment, she hadn't thought of what she would do if Charles refused to see her. Would she leave, humiliated, or make a scene and refuse to leave? But her fears were relieved a second later, when the receptionist told her, "He says you can go inside."

Gathering all of her courage, Adina opened the door to Charles's office and, without even pausing to look at him, turned to close it behind her, before she confronted him.

"Well, well, well!" Charles started before Adina could say a word. "Look who we have here! If it's not the Queen of Sheba herself! What brings you to this side of town, your royal highness? It better be a millennium worthy goal, because the UN could use some new ideas!"

"Hi, Charles, how are you?" Adina simply said. She didn't want to give him a chance to rant and rave any longer than he already had.

"I'm fine, *my wife*; thanks for asking! Mwahahaha!" he said, laughing his most annoying, narcissistic laugh, which Adina had come to hate. He always told her he was her first, and he would be her last; reminding her that she was a virgin when he met her. It always got on Adina's last nerve. But on this day, she tried to ignore what he said and focus on why she came to see him.

"Listen, I don't want to waste your time, or mine. That's why I came during the lunch hour. I wanted to talk to you about the kids." Adina wanted to spell it out and leave as soon as possible.

"Kids? What kids? Yours or mine?" Charles knew all his ex-wife's fragile buttons and when to press them. That's why Adina had given up asking for his support for the kids. She hated how he belittled her with sadistic rants. He never forgot to bring up her childhood abandonment issues, her white adoptive parents, or the fact that she didn't have any known relatives she could call her family.

"I mean, you were raised by white folks, so I guess you're not as African as the rest of us. Do you think you're superior, or better than other Africans or black folk?" Charles used to say during their heated arguments when they were married.

Adina's heart ached in her chest as she remembered the terrible things Charles used to say to her. His verbal abuse had become her worst nightmare. She had tried to forgive him, but some words just left wounds on one's heart, and she didn't know how to erase that recording from her mind.

"Charles, please! Listen first, and you can make your sarcastic comments after. Please?" Adina said, trying to appear calmer and composed than she felt. She didn't want to lose ground in front of him or at his workplace—at least not now. She could deal with her emotions over the meeting in her own space and time after she got home.

"Okay, okay. I'm all ears, madam." He gestured for her to sit down across from him. He looked intensely in Adina's eyes, as if he wanted a staring contest; which made her uncomfortable, but she decided she had to be strong for her kids.

"So, what is it that couldn't wait until the end of the day?" Charles was about to start haranguing her, but Adina cut him off.

"It's about my…it's my job. I lost my job; the organization is in some kind of downsizing phase." She couldn't tell him that she had been fired. She already knew what he would say if he knew she was fired. So, she had decided to lie to him. But she wasn't a good liar, and as soon as she said it, she looked away.

"Um…I'm sorry to hear that, I think!" Charles said. Adina couldn't believe he could pronounce the word "sorry."

"Thank you," Adina said, but she wasn't prepared for what came next.

"How are the kids? And how are you otherwise?" Charles asked. Adina wasn't sure whether he meant it or not. After their two years of divorce, and his ignoring her and the kids, she had come to the conclusion that he didn't care about them, or want them in his life. Certainly, coming to talk to him about the kids today wasn't going to change anything; Adina was sure of that.

"The kids are alright, and I'm fine too. What about you?" Adina replied. She could see something in Charles 'eye, but she wasn't sure whether it was remorse, or just fatigue. And she wasn't going to ask him. She still hadn't told him why she had come to see him at work.

"Charles, you know I hate fighting with you, or with anybody for that matter. I'm just not a good fighter, and I've accepted that. Today is no exception. I didn't come to fight with you; I only came to ask you to help with the kids. I don't have the financial means to take care of three kids by myself in New York City, and you know how expensive this city is. So, please, you need to increase the child support, and cover more of the kids' expenses."

Adina was almost pleading her case; she knew she had no other alternative. She needed his help, and she could no longer let him off the hook when it came to his fatherly responsibilities. This situation had gone on for far too long, and Charles had become comfortable with the arrangement. Adina knew he loved not being responsible for anyone but himself. She was sure he would not like her now telling him to change that and become involved in his kids' lives.

"Oh, okay! I get it!" Charles replied. "So, now that Ms. Ethiopia cannot seduce men into giving her a job, she comes crawling to her ex-husband she threw out of the house two years ago?"

Charles said it with venom in his eyes, causing Adina's first tears to run down her high cheekbones. She wished she could stop them, but she couldn't. Charles's words hurt her beyond description, and reopened all the raw wounds of their relationship. During their marriage, he had always accused her of seducing men, even though he was the one sleeping around.

"Charles, you know what? Keep it; keep your money. The kids and I will survive; we are in God's hands, not yours."

Adina's voice broke as she spoke, but she managed to say it all, and then she stormed out of Charles's office and headed to the elevator.

"Adina, wait! Come back for goodness sake," Charles said, running after her to the elevator. "I was just joking; did you lose your sense of humor too when you lost your job? Baby, wait!"

"Don't you ever baby me!" Adina said angrily. She hated that she couldn't hold in her anger because it just showed him how he could upset her.

"Okay, okay, Adina; let's go back to my office and talk, please!" Charles insisted.

Adina could see that he meant it, but she hated herself even more for agreeing to go back into his office. She understood now how easy it was for women to go back to their abusive exes; such men were good at manipulating others. But, she owed it to her kids, and so, she swallowed her pride and walked back with him to his office.

"Adina, baby," he started again as soon as they were both seated with the door closed.

"I'm not your baby," she said, almost adding, *Call that your bimbos*, but she didn't dare say it.

"I will help," Charles simply said.

"What?" Adina asked in a low voice. She didn't want to get her hopes up, and have them crashed in the next minute.

Charles was capable of ping-pong-ing her emotions back and forth, and she knew she had allowed it for too long.

"I will give you more money for the children, but we have to make the deal between ourselves. No lawyers or court can be involved." Charles said in a bossy voice.

Adina took a deep breath; she felt her diaphragm starting to knot, and she slowly exhaled.

"There is a condition, though!" Charles added. "We will meet twice a week at my place and have hot sex, just like we used to do, huh? Remember the good old days?"

Adina felt nauseated and ready to throw up.

"So, that's what it was for you—hot sex?" Adina spat out. "I thought we were making love; you had hot sex with your bimbos, not me."

Adina could hear her friend Aleah encouraging her in the moment. "Oh, no, you didn't!" Aleah would urge her. "Tell him, girl; get it out of your system…. Damn!"

Adina couldn't believe she had said that to him. It was the first time she had used the word *bimbo* to his face. For a moment, she was sure she was going to walk out with another punched face. But Charles became quiet.

He looked down at his hands and said, "I deserve it. Go ahead; punch me in the gut and get your revenge."

"I don't want to get a revenge, Charles; I just wish you had a conscience," she said, now letting all her emotions loose. "I wish you'd just say you were sorry for once for all the pain you've put me and the kids through! Your kids don't even get to see you; it's as if you're dead and they don't have a father. I was an orphan, but I later had parents who loved me very much. Even though they are dead now, I still feel their presence all the time. I also feel the presence of my mother, who was shunned by society because she had a baby out of wedlock at sixteen. I used to feel like I was the cause of her shame, and the shame of her entire family I don't even know. Maybe if I weren't born, she would still be alive. But I've come to the realization that I was born for a purpose. I was a blessing to a couple who could not have kids of their own."

Adina paused to take a breath and then continued, "You and I have been blessed with three kids, but you've abandoned them, Charles. What kind of human being are you?"

Adina was on fire. She couldn't stop. She had bottled up all of these painful emotions for too long; they had to come out.

"When my new mom and dad adopted me, they gave me a better life. But I was already screwed up on the inside. I had abandonment issues, and I longed for a family that didn't exist, a father whom I never knew, and will never know. I thought by marrying you I could have that family I longed for, but, you, Charles, you…." She stopped and wiped her tears before continuing as Charles sat silent.

"You cut me off from the chance of knowing your parents; you hate your father, and you never gave our children a chance to be spoiled by their grandparents. Who are you, Charles Kumi? You're a monster and a selfish snob. You know what, Charles? Keep your money. I'm not a whore you can pay to have sex with. I don't want your money. Keep it and take it with you to your grave."

After Adina had said all she felt, she stormed out of the office and arrived at the elevator just as its door was closing. She entered and quickly closed the door before Charles could follow her. Once she was back in the lobby, she ran out of the building to the tramway. She was back home by quarter after two.

. . . .

Two weeks after Adina's fight with her ex-husband, she was surprised to receive an envelope in the mail with his return address on it. Inside was a check for $5,000 and a letter of apology, in which he stated his regrets and that he was sorry for not being the husband she deserved, or a good father to their kids. Adina was grateful for the check and the apology. After a little thought, she decided to call and thank him. She told him she forgave him, and he promised to make an effort to be more involved in their kids' lives.

Later that month, Charles called Adina in a distraught voice. His father, Reverend Kumi, had passed away from a heart attack the night before; he was eighty-six years old. When Charles called Adina, he asked her to go with him to the funeral in Detroit and she agreed. They drove to Syracuse University to pick Bella up, and the whole family drove to Michigan for the funeral. Charles sobbed uncontrollably when he hugged his mother. Adina could see years of regret in his eyes. Not being able to forgive his father for what he had perceived as injustice toward him when he was growing up weighed on Charles's heart. It was a lesson for Adina as well. So, she decided to forgive Charles for the pain he had inflicted on her, and to stop carrying the heavy burden for things she couldn't change in him.

Sometimes, God brings two broken souls together for a reason. Adina had been broken by abandonment issues from a young age. Charles had been broken by his own resentment toward his father. Now, perhaps, Adina thought, they could be friends and heal some of their mutual pain.

CHAPTER 8

As much as Adina thought she had tried to heal the emotional wounds caused by her divorce, there was another kind of healing she needed to complete; and that was to trust another man in her life. Even Geneva liked to ask her whether she would ever get married again. Adina didn't know what to say about that. She knew she liked a steady family life, but with all she had been through with Charles, she didn't want to risk her heart again. She told herself time and again that she had been there and done that. She felt there was no need for a man in her life because it was not worth the risk of being hurt again. Charles's mistreatment of her had only accentuated her feelings of rejection, and she did not think she could bear to experience that kind of rejection again.

In middle school, to escape her feelings of being different from her classmates, Adina had begun indulging in reading. In high school, she started losing herself in books to keep her mind from wandering too much into her painful past. She read romance novels that mirrored her own life, but with a happy ending.

She also loved to write short stories, and she had always wondered what it would be like to write a book. Whenever she had free time, especially when she was bored or sad, or both, Adina would write in her journals, which had accumulated over the years. Her mother had always encouraged her to write as a means of healing whatever bothered her at the time. For Adina, writing allowed her to express her pain from not knowing who her biological parents had been, or the fact that she felt like an outcast in school.

Later, in the workplace, the outcast feeling hadn't subsided, so she wrote at night before going to sleep. Now, as a divorcée, Adina distracted herself from her emotions by focusing on her kids' activities and her own writing when the kids were not home. When it came to romance, Adina had built a wall and settled behind it. She loved her children so much that she told herself they were more than enough to fill her life with happiness. But, at times, she fantasized about what kind of man she wanted in her life, not believing such a man could exist. She wanted a man who would be there for her and her children, someone who would love her unconditionally, with all her baggage. "Girl," she would then tease herself when she caught herself daydreaming, "fantasies are just that—fantasies! Not reality, but only daydreaming!"

It had been three years since Adina had been with a man, and that man had been Charles when she was still married to him. After Adina's divorce, Aleah had tried to hook her up with single men, but Adina always refused. Once, Aleah had come to visit Adina with Danny, a man in his forties, who taught in the same school district where Aleah worked. At Aleah's insistence, Adina had agreed to go out with Danny one time—and that was enough for her. Danny had never been married, and he wanted the world to revolve only around him. He did not want to share his woman's attention with any kids, and he told her so. Adina didn't blame him; not everyone could handle a woman with a bundle of kids. They had mutually decided to break off the relationship, before it even started, so, no one was hurt.

Adina needed a man who could be a father figure in her kids' lives, and she didn't want to compromise on that, no matter how lonely she felt. She knew finding such a man was an exception rather than the rule—basically, an impossibility. And she was okay with that, at least most of the time.

Despite Adina's aversion to dating, her friends didn't relent. They fixed her up with blind dates, speed dating, and other venues where she could meet men. On the third anniversary of her divorce, Adina agreed to go with her newly divorced friend, Carrie, to a singles' event in New Jersey. That's when Carrie introduced her to online dating, which sounded like a horrible experience in Adina's opinion. She thought it was for desperate people, but she soon discovered she had become one of them when she set up her profile on loveme.com, a dating website that promised to match people with likable wannabe daters.

The day she decided to sign up, Adina made sure she hid all the dating websites she had viewed to avoid being tracked by her kids. She doubted her kids would ever check the websites she had viewed, but she could just imagine them stumbling on one by accident and saying, "Mom, you went on a dating website?" and looking at her with suspicious teenage eyes. The website Carrie advised her to sign up with, loveme.com, had a slogan that said, "Meeting your fine match is just a matter of a mouse click." As she entered her personal information, she felt as if someone were watching over her shoulder, shaking his head disapprovingly. She could just hear her ex-husband's condescending tone, telling her, "Well, well, well, look who's desperate now?" She almost broke her computer screen as she slammed it shut.

Reluctantly, an hour later, Adina returned to her computer, only to hear again Charles's same voice saying, "Really, Adina? That's what you've resorted to? Why don't you just come to Papa! Mwahahaha...!" She tried to ignore the voice, but feelings of shame overwhelmed her, so she gave up.

Adina concluded that this online dating business wasn't for her. Once again, she struggled with thoughts of shame, guilt, and the whole shebang of negative emotions. She almost called her ex-husband to ask him if he would please take her back. But instead, she called Carrie.

"Carrie, I can't do it!"

"Uhh... you can't do what?" Carrie asked.

"This online dating, Carrie! This is not for me! I can't put myself out there in cyberspace; it's so humiliating! Plus, I keep hearing Charles's disapproving voice, making narcissistic comments."

"Aahh...we got ex-husband issues! Honey, that's normal the first time you think of dating another man. Those are normal feelings; every woman goes through them when she gets back out there! How else are you going to meet a man? This is the new and best way to meet a vast pool of men, and then to choose the ones you want to test out to see whom you like. You can't just buy a dress without trying it on for size, can you now?"

Listening to Carrie, Adina had the clear impression her friend had tested out a few men, but she wasn't going to do that. Just the thought of going to bed with another man left her nauseous. Especially if that man was someone she met online. "Yuck…" was her reaction to Carrie's statement.

Carrie kept telling her own online dating success stories. She was now dating a TV producer from Jersey Shore, whom she was crazy in love with, and they had met on the same dating site Carrie had told Adina to sign up with.

Adina waited another week before she convinced herself to try signing up again. She had taken time to think about the pros and cons of online dating, and she had decided to give it a try at her friend's insistence. The hardest thing was setting up her profile. She felt impatient as she filled out the long questionnaire. It was like answering job interview questions rather than going on a love quest. The questions where she had to talk about herself were the hardest. On the one hand, she didn't want to brag too much about herself; on the other hand, she seemed to lack much to brag about, and that concerned her. Talking about herself had never been easy for Adina. She knew she needed to give an optimistic view of her life, so she wouldn't frighten away her potential matches. But having lost her job and having no steady income to take care of herself and her children, she didn't feel perky. Nonetheless, she decided to give it a try.

"Who cares if I'm not exactly where I want to be in life." She could even lie about herself, since this was online where no one could verify the information she shared. But, Adina wasn't a good liar, not even online. Where appropriate, instead of lying, she withheld the optional information to make sure she didn't scare off her love prospects.

The next day, when Adina logged on to the dating website, she already had more than ninety potential dating matches waiting for her to review. *My, oh my!* She had mixed feelings. One part of her wanted to withdraw her profile right away, to run and hide. Another part of her, stronger than she expected, was curious and wanted to review every one of her alleged matches. She sat down and browsed through her matches' profiles, giving them equal opportunity reviewing time.

The next day, she profusely studied each one of her matches, the photo-less profiles as well as those with photos. Talking about pictures, she saw an interesting variety; some overwhelmingly not so good. Besides the usual blurriness that one could expect from uploading photos, one man's profile picture showed hair sticking out of his nose. Others posted photos taken with Grandma the day she turned 105. In the latter, Adina wasn't sure whether her match wanted her to date him or Grandma because, sometimes, she couldn't tell whom the one with the mustache was!

Other matches, eager to show their loving sides, posted their pictures of themselves holding younger women, attractive in most cases, without bothering to caption whether the women were their dear daughters or ex-wives. It was a confusing time for Adina.

After a couple of days of going through these profiles, Adina was already discouraged. She waited to see whether her matches would initiate or communicate with her. But no one sent her a word. How come other people found love online, like Carrie, but she couldn't? Carrie had made it sound too simple and fun. No one had ever told her it would take this long. (It had been four days already.)

When self-doubt crept in, Adina began reviewing her own profile to determine whether she was, indeed, dating material. She reviewed it several times to see whether she would date herself, if she were a man. But all she could see in her profile were flaws, starting with her picture, and then the answers to the questions. She posted a different picture, changed the answers in her profile, tried to be cute here and there, cut a sentence out, changed an adjective, and found a better qualifier. Again, there was still no communication from her matches. Then, she posted a second picture and upgraded her profile—yet again.

Overjoyed in her belief that she had gotten it right this time, Adina decided to let her profile sit for a couple of days. In the meantime, she kept receiving more profile matches from the website database. Still, none of her matches initiated any communication—not even a wink! Then, she called Carrie to report how excruciating this experience was for her.

"You have to be proactive, Adina," Carrie reassured her. "Men can be intimidated, too, and they like to see that you're interested! This is America, baby, and it's the twenty-first century. Women can initiate dating, duhhh! Why wait for the men to do all the work?"

With Carrie's encouragement, Adina decided to send a few winks to some of her matches. Then, she started sending enthusiastic messages: "Just read your profile and just wanted to say hi!" Some did respond, with restraint; others just winked back. And then, one day Adina received a "Would like to get to know you" message. She jumped out of her chair. Someone was interested in her after all?

The next day, she was ready for some online romance with her "new man." She checked the message he had sent her and carefully prepared a smart reply. She was almost planning a wedding when, after she entered his user name to bring up his profile, the website let her know that the user could not be found. *What?* She tried to bring up his profile again, making sure there was no typo this time. The system replied, "User not found." First, Adina was disappointed. *He likes me; now he likes me not?* She thought. Second, she was horrified. *Could it be that I was communicating with a scammer, a creep, a pedophile, a criminal?* And finally, she was empathetic. *Maybe he's out of a job like me, and couldn't pay for the membership fee.*

A week later, she thought, *Maybe he's married and his wife caught him cheating online.* Oh well, whatever the reason, Adina got over him after just a week. She gave herself a pat on the back. "Good one, kiddo! You can't even find a man online."

Yes, her ego was bruised—a little! But she had survived worse blows in her life. She started to view this online dating thing as an adventure, just as Carrie kept telling her.

"Honey, do it as an adventure, to get out of your comfort zone."

Adina was not a risk-taker, and she knew it. And she also knew that whenever one embarked on an adventure, there were rewards, as well as a few bumps along the way. The road to any type of success was paved with a few stops, detours, and wrong turns.

The old Adina would have canceled her online dating membership after finding a good reason for her fear of risk-taking. But the "new Adina," as her friends urged her to become, decided to stick around at least until her membership expired.

She had to revisit her expectations and be clear about what she wanted. She decided to stay at least for the exercise and develop some dating muscle. She also looked at it as an opportunity for self-discovery. What were her needs versus her yearnings? This time, when Adina updated her profile, it was in the spirit of promoting a strong, beautiful, and intelligent Adina—not someone desperate to meet a mate. In truth, she wasn't desperate. *Okay, maybe a little*, she thought. But there was no need to beat herself up, as she usually did. In the end, she learned to be more compassionate toward herself.

When her online dating membership expired after three months, Adina decided not to renew it. But that decision wasn't fear-based this time. After she realized how many people were posting their dating profiles online, in the quest for the elusive *one*, she understood that humanity was really one people across all races and cultures. Everyone wanted the same—to be loved for their true selves. She certainly hoped that one day she would meet a man who would love her for who she was, baggage and all. Someone who would offer her the companionship she longed for—someone who would extend to her a hand to hold.

CHAPTER 9

Ever since she had been fired, Adina had searched for other jobs, but to no avail. Every day, she scanned job ads in newspapers and on the Internet. She applied for many positions, but nothing turned up as quickly as she wished or needed. The only job she was offered was located on Long Island, an hour-and-a-half commute each way, and she didn't want to do that to her kids, especially Haile. After reevaluating the job's requirements and the commute time, she turned it down. Other job possibilities seemed to be for a similar position to the one she had been fired from, specifying the skills wanted as: "advanced knowledge of Excel, working under pressure, unlimited flexibility," and other requirements that Adina knew she didn't want to commit to. She didn't want to repeat the scenario of her previous job, which she had never liked anyway. Plus, it had taken her months to get over the ordeal of being fired. This time, she didn't want just any job; it would have to be work she would truly enjoy, allowing her to use her creative energy. But that type of work was nowhere to be found.

In the meantime, as she always did when she was younger, Adina found joy in books. She read insatiably, both fiction and nonfiction. She loved to read novels with stories that seemed realistic and mirrored her own life in some ways. She also loved the world of fantasy romance, with characters whose lives were too good to be true, of course, but they took her mind off her own troubles. For nonfiction, she read mostly memoirs and self-help books that were inspiring and gave her a daily boost.

She also loved writing to kill time while waiting for another job. Her most cherished piece of writing was her memoir, which she had written after she got divorced from Charles. It had been both therapeutic and a journey of self-discovery. She had worked on it day and night; whenever she found alone time. She would go to the library and write there for hours, and also write at night when the kids went to sleep. It had taken her only six months to finish, and she wished she could get it published, but she didn't know how. She had a ready-to-go manuscript, but she had not shown it to anyone. She had told Aleah about her writing, but her friend was more of a hands-on person and less dreamy. Aleah called writing, "fantasy art" and saw it as a hobby, not a real job that could sustain a family.

"Honey, you need a real day job; you can write your heart out when you're retired." Aleah repeatedly told Adina. Adina knew her best friend meant well; Aleah was more realistic than she was, but Aleah didn't have the intense burning desire to write that Adina had.

Adina had learned at a young age to write as a way of filling the void she felt in her heart—first, as an adopted child when she had felt lonely with no siblings to play with at home. And then, in grade school, where she mostly felt different, and her classmates never missed reminding her that she was. So, she learned to create characters in her head, and later, writing became her time away from every pain she experienced. The characters Adina created resembled her own life, and she invented scenarios on how to get through their hurdles of pain and heartache. So, when she started working on her memoir, it was easy for her because she had written it as fiction first, but now she had decided to share her true story.

Adina started educating herself about how to get published, and in the process, she read that most first-time authors didn't get published, because they had no known work to their credit.

"Duh...how are we supposed to get our work known if we're not given a chance to get published in the first place?" Adina whined to herself one day, as she read how to submit publishing queries.

She wanted a chance to share her life story with the world, but first- time authors' books were not hot cupcakes to publishing houses. It saddened Adina that she couldn't find a venue for the one thing she was committed to doing, and the only activity that filled her life with joy and purpose—her writing.

Adina had put her manuscript away after many edits, and started writing short stories. She had even entered writing contests to gain exposure, and two of her short stories had won prizes in fiction categories. She had written a good number of stories before, and one day, she decided to send some to literary agents, thinking perhaps she could publish a short story collection. After a couple of rejections, which of course she took personally, she received a letter from the Neman Literary Agency.

Dear Ms. Springfield,

Thank you for your recent submission. I like your writing voice; however, I'm more interested in novels than short stories."

Sincerely yours,

Ben Neman

After reading the note, Adina felt a strong urge to call the agency. Before she could change her mind, she picked up the phone and called the number written on the letterhead. Her hands shook as she dialed and waited for someone to pick up. Knowing that Ben Neman, the head of the literary agency, *liked her writing voice,* raised something in Adina's spirit. She desperately needed confirmation that she wasn't as stupid as she thought she was.

"Neman Literary Agency, Ben here; who's this?" said a deep voice on the other end of the line.

Adina was surprised that Ben would pick up the phone himself and not a secretary, but she took it as a good sign to continue.

"Oh, hello, Mr. Neman? This is uuh…Adina—Adina Springfield." Adina had never felt comfortable saying her last name since it belonged to her adoptive parents. She felt as if it were borrowed from them, and was not the last name she should have. She had taken her husband's last name when they got married, but after the divorce, she had decided to go back to Springfield to honor her adoptive parents. But it still felt awkward to her whenever people addressed her by it.

"Yes, how can I help you, Ms. Springfield?"

He didn't sound overly friendly, so Adina suspected he didn't recognize her name.

"Uhm…you sent me a note about a short story I submitted to you. And you said you liked…I mean, liked my writing voice?" Adina almost whispered.

"What did you say your name was again?" Ben asked.

"Adina Springfield," she replied, trying to stay calmer than she really felt. She didn't know why, but Ben's booming voice sounded intriguing and even reassuring to her ears. She had to fight to stay focused on the conversation and not let her mind wander.

"Oh, yes! I remember now! You're the one with that 'Wisdom of the Geese' story?" Ben made it sound like a half-question, half-confirmation. "So, what's up with the story? Did you get anybody to publish it?"

"No, I haven't yet, but I've been thinking about what you said...I mean in your note." Adina felt embarrassed to sound almost clingy.

"Okay, what have you been thinking about?" Ben asked.

Adina was surprised he would continue to talk to her, but she realized this could be her only chance.

As if she were walking on water, fighting for balance, Adina carefully said, "I was thinking that maybe I could write a book as you said in your note, and...—"

"Absolutely. I, too, think you should, Ms. Springfield!" Ben interjected before she could finish.

"Adina. Please call me Adina."

"All right, Adina." The name *Adina* sounded sticky when he said it. "Why don't we meet and discuss it over a cup of coffee since we live in the same vicinity?"

Adina was surprised by his offer, but her woman's intuition made her wonder why he didn't ask to meet her in his office. However, she reasoned with herself that maybe that's how the publishing business worked. Adina didn't understand why she was fretting about meeting a male agent. She kept reminding herself that agents do come in all genders! And the meeting was about business, not a blind date. After all these thoughts quickly ran through her head, she decided this was her chance to get an entrance into the publishing world. So, she said, "Yes, I would like that. Thank you."

"Okay, how about Tuesday then?" Ben asked.

They agreed on a time and a place to meet. After the call ended, Adina thought he had sounded so genuine and professional that she felt silly to have thought he could be some kind of womanizer. "Girl, get it together, and get a grip for goodness' sake!" she laughed at herself. Maybe the reason she was tripping was because she hadn't had sex since her divorce. But she needed an agent, and apparently, Ben was proving to be the agent she needed. And that was that! She didn't need to censor every encounter in her "not-so-wonderful" life.

"Why would a literary agent want me when he can have all the famous people in the world?" Adina kept asking herself, but, she made an effort to chill. Why was she assuming it would be anything other than a business meeting? Adina put her two hands on her heart and slowly breathed in and out to soothe her mind from wandering too much. Then, she went to the supermarket to pick up a few groceries before her kids came home from school.

. . . .

Ben lived in lower Manhattan, and his agency had been successful mainly by helping new writers who went on to become number one *New York Times'* bestsellers. He had a gift of compassion for the stories he represented, so he was more inclined than most agents to help what he called "the non- celebs." Those were writers who were not known, and would normally have no chance of getting their books published. He stayed away from celebrities' books because they didn't have any trouble finding publishers. He had represented some politicians' biographies, but only if he thought they were inspiring for the average Joe. He wanted meaningful stories that helped others to better their lives.

On Tuesday, when Adina went to meet Ben, she had an outline and a brief summary of each chapter of her memoir. As she entered the café where Ben was waiting, she looked like a lost child in the London Subway system. There was only one man in the café, so, she knew it had to be Ben. He was a handsome white man, with a Mediterranean tan, very masculine looking, with curly black hair. He had to be 6'5", Adina estimated. He was wearing a dark gray suit, with a blue shirt and a matching tie. He looked like a Fortune 500 company CEO, rather than a literary agent. Adina became even more nervous as she thought about her memoir; her life story was filled with drama. She felt she had nothing glamorous to present to this man. She almost turned back when she saw Ben approaching her.

"Hello, I'm Benjamin Neman. You must be Ms. Springfield?" Ben said, extending his hand.

"Hi. It's a pleasure to meet you, Mr. Neman." As Adina shook his hand, she felt heat all over her body, as she realized she was trembling at the knee level. She had worn her all-time conservative black skirt, and a matching jacket, over a pink shirt, and she had tied her curly long hair into a knot with a big hair clipper. Ben directed her to a quiet corner where he had ordered a cup of coffee. Adina sat down, and set her leather folder containing the outline beside her.

"Would you like some coffee?" Ben asked her.

"Yes, actually, I'd like tea, please. Thank you," she said, nervously touching her fingers. And right then, she noticed Ben was eyeing her fingers to see whether she was wearing a wedding band. Since she was not wearing one, he would now know she was single.

"I didn't know they had tea in New York!" Ben teased her. She realized he must see how nervous she was, and was trying to lighten up the atmosphere. She imagined most new authors were nervous when embarking on the publishing adventure, and he would know that.

For a fraction of a second, Adina lost focus and checked Ben's fingers for a ring as well. She saw none, but she quickly landed back on planet Earth. She remembered that some men hid their wedding bands in their pockets, when they went on business trips. Her ex-husband had done it many times before she found out he was cheating on her. Maybe that's what Ben was doing, too. If this man were a player, she decided she would spit in his face and run. Well, that's what Aleah would do, but not her. She didn't have the backbone.

"Is your family here in New York?" Ben asked. She realized it was a two-layer question, but she only answered one layer.

"Yes, my family is here in New York." Ben must not have been impressed by the short answer because he pressed further.

"You know, husband, kids—the whole bundle?"

Adina's face stood erect when the word "husband" was mentioned. Then her neck became stiff, before her shoulders slugged, and she felt a mist of sweat on her hands. Adina hated to talk about being divorced, especially to people who didn't know her.

"Yes. They live with me, I mean…um…the kids live with me." She said it as if she had been asked to recite the Ten Commandments, and state which one she had breached.

But Ben replied, "I'm twice divorced, so…no judging!" When he laughed, Adina relaxed.

"Yeah, me too…I mean, once divorced. You still beat me, though!" Adina said smiling.

"Sooo…how many kids do you have? You said you live with your kids?" Ben asked.

So much for a business meeting, Adina thought to herself. This was turning too personal. But, wasn't a memoir exactly that? A personal story? He had a right to know a little more about her life if he were going to represent her work to publishers.

She steadied herself and answered, "Three." Anything that involved talking about her kids lit up her face.

He smiled and asked, "Ages?"

Boy, he did want to know about her personal life!

"Well, for starters, Bella is twenty-one and a junior at Syracuse. Geneva is seventeen and a senior in high school, and Haile is twelve and in seventh grade."

"Good grace! You have a twenty-one-year old? You look so young yourself! I would never imagine you have a twenty-one-year-old child," Ben said.

"I was two when I had my first child, so…" Adina said, as she took a sip of her tea and laughed.

"And that makes you…let's see…twenty-three, right?" Ben asked.

"Yep, and I can start drinking too!" she replied, and they both laughed.

"I'm starving; would you like to eat something?" Ben asked.

"That would be nice!" Adina hadn't eaten anything that morning. She had been so anxious to meet her prospective literary agent that she had forgotten to eat breakfast. The tea she was drinking at the café was making her hungrier.

The café-restaurant Ben had chosen was lovely, more suitable for romantic dates than meeting your literary agent. After they ordered lunch, Ben got down to business.

"So, do you have anything in your leather folder that you'd like to show me? You're too protective of it; it must be your favorite child. Does your son know about this other baby?" Ben teased.

Adina opened the folder nervously, as if the content might roll out of it and escape.

"It's nothing. Just some rough ideas of what I would like to write about. Nothing as glamorous as what you're probably used to."

"Do you mind if I take a look?" Ben asked.

Adina almost didn't let him. She felt so embarrassed that she had promised she could write a book, but now that she was sitting with a "real" literary agent, she wasn't sure she had the talent to write a book, or whether what she had written could be called a book.

"I promise to return this precious child of yours to you right away," Ben assured her.

Adina took the papers out of the folder and carefully placed them on the table in front of Ben. He dipped his hand in his pocket, and took out his reading glasses; then he silently started reading. He read the summary first, and then the chapter headings. In all, it took him about seven minutes, before he talked to Adina again, which seemed like infinity to her. She had opened a magazine and feigned reading it, but she only saw a blur. She was so anxious, and the silence was becoming unbearable. The more Ben focused on reading her book outline, the more uncomfortable Adina felt. It was as if she were naked in front of a stranger. Knowing that this man was learning about her personal life embarrassed her deeply. Adina couldn't believe she had let him read the summary of her story.

Right when Ben finished reading Adina's book outline, their lunch came. After the waitress finished setting the food on the table, she asked them whether they needed anything else before she disappeared into the kitchen. But, Adina was no longer hungry. All she wanted was to get out of there, go home and hide. She didn't even want to hear his feedback because she knew she wasn't a "writer." *Please, who am I trying to impress?* she silently scolded herself.

As far as Adina was concerned, she was a failure at everything, and she accepted that. The last thing she needed was to hear it from someone else. The only real accomplishment of her life had been having and raising her kids. At least, she gave herself permission for praise when it came to her children. Other than that, she had pretty much failed. Not that she hadn't tried—but she had made peace with it.

When Ben turned to look at her after his first bite into his sandwich, she was almost a wreck.

"Young lady, what are we going to do with you?" he said first.

Oh, God, he hated it! Adina thought, *and now he's going to tell me I'm a complete failure.* She wasn't looking forward to another rejection. She had had enough of those.

"I love it!" Ben continued excitedly.

Adina just stared at him, almost emotionless.

"What did you just say?" Adina thought she had lost her mind. She couldn't believe she had heard him right.

"I said…*you, young lady, are a great writer!*" Ben said, emphasizing every word. "Do I need to put it in writing?" he continued teasingly.

Adina was so shocked by his words that she began to cry. Oh, God! Tears were spreading along her cheeks and washing away the little mascara she had applied. Someone loved her book outline? Someone didn't call her a failure like she had come to think of herself when it came to her professional resume and career? After all, she had nothing to show for her years in college and the huge student loan she still hadn't paid off.

Ben gave her a napkin to wipe her tears. Now she was embarrassed for crying in front of a stranger, and not just any stranger—a successful literary agent who happened to like her writing.

Ben stopped eating and asked, "Are you okay? Did I say something wrong?"

"Yes…I mean no. Not something wrong." She could see how carefully he was staring at her, as if he really cared about how she was feeling.

"So, what's wrong?" he asked. "I thought you'd be happy to hear that you're a great writer? Now, understand, I'm not saying I will publish your work; we will have to see how your manuscript turns out. I'm just giving you feedback based on your outline."

"Yes, yes, I know. But you said you love it!" Adina said between breaths. *I'm definitely heading toward menopause, or mid-life crisis, or both*, she thought to herself.

"And that's not good?" Ben asked. "Should I hate it? You should have told me."

Ben was trying to lighten the mood. He understood her emotions. He had been there himself as a first-time writer, and later as an agent meeting new writers from all walks of life.

"I am happy that you love it!" Adina replied. "I was afraid you would hate it, and say that it was baloney." Adina was now laughing through her tears. She reached into her purse for some tissues, blew her nose, and dried her eyes. Then she picked at her lunch, which had gone cold, but she was now too happy to eat.

"Yes, I love it," Ben repeated. "I think you have talent, Adina; raw, dormant talent that is still virgin and needs to be explored and dug out. May I see the outline again, please?"

"Oh, my God; I'm so happy right now! You have no idea," said Adina, quickly giving him back the outline. "Thank you, so, so much for your time."

He looked over it a bit more and made important suggestions as they finished eating. Then, as they stood up to leave, Adina thanked him again profusely, and he promised he would find her the best publisher to publish her memoir.

"I work with a lot of brilliant publishing houses and will find you the right fit for your work."

Then Ben surprised her by saying, "Adina, I'm also interested in you."

"Interested in me? What are you talking about?" Adina said with a little confusion in her eyes; but then it dawned on her.

"I knew it! I knew you weren't interested in my book. What was I thinking?" Adina sat down again and started to cry fresh tears.

"Adina, I'm sorry. I didn't mean to upset you. I…I am interested in your writing; of course, I am! But I also feel attracted to you."

Adina became visibly troubled by Ben's announcement—and very upset.

"Really! Interested in me?" Adina exclaimed. "Is that your best pick-up line? You don't even know me, but you're attracted to me? Who do you think I am? Some poor African woman you can just take advantage of because she's a single mother?"

Adina actually felt kind of better letting out her anger, but she was also somewhat embarrassed by her own reaction. It was almost 3:45 p.m., and no one else was in the café, except the owner who was busy with his kitchen. Adina sat quietly for a moment, waiting for Ben to tell her off and leave.

Instead, Ben said, "Adina, please, listen to me. I'm not trying to take advantage of you. I know we just met, but I like you. I really do. Maybe using the word 'attracted' at the first encounter was over the top, especially at a business meeting. I am sorry about my lousy vocabulary. But I really like you. In fact, I think you're the most beautiful woman I've ever met. I promise I won't hurt you, Adina."

She could see his pleading eyes, but she still had to know whether or not he was sincere.

"Please, Adina, go on a date with me! That's all I'm asking. Just one date, this once; and if after that you don't want to see me again, I will respect that. You have my word," Ben continued.

"So, you're not 'attracted' to me anymore. Now you only 'like' me?" Adina started, jokingly before adding, "Okay, just one time, and it's not a date!"

She laughed as she blew her nose again because it sounded stuffy, as if she had a cold. She was sorry her emotional rollercoaster was taking a toll on this man she had just met. In her heart of hearts, she knew he probably meant well.

They stood up and went outside. He offered to give her a ride home, but she thought that might be moving too fast. When he gave her his business card, she wrote her phone number on the back and returned it to him—a sign of trust. Still, she did agree to meet him for a real date that weekend, when her kids would be staying at their father's, now that Charles had become more involved in his kids' lives.

As Adina walked to the tramway to go home, she thought how she had never met anyone like Ben, and she liked him too—a lot—although she didn't want to admit it. She felt eager for the weekend to come when she would see him again. Despite her resistance to dating, she felt she could trust Ben. Even though she often wanted to stay away from men, she felt lonely most of the time, and like everyone else, she craved companionship.

When Adina got home, Geneva was listening to music on the computer, ears plugged with earphones, while doing her homework. Adina took out her folder and read the comments Ben had made on her book's outline. She was so deep into reading the comments that she even forgot to hug her daughter.

"What's up, Mom?" Geneva asked when she noticed her mother had returned. She hadn't heard her come in because of the music blasting through her earphones. "You don't hug me anymore? Where were you anyway?"

Geneva was her mother's biggest teaser. Adina didn't want to worry her children about her getting involved with another man, before she herself felt comfortable with the idea. She needed lots and lots of time to determine Ben would be the one, before she would introduce him to her children.

Before Adina could think what to reply, Geneva teased, "Were you out with a cute guy, Ma? Seriously, I think you should date. How long has it been since you and dad got divorced? Three years? Definitely, you should find yourself a man!"

"Geneva, I'm not a teenager anymore," said Adina, feeling defensive because her daughter almost seemed to know what she had been up to. "You girls think a man is everything?"

"Everything? Pleeease! Speak for yourself. I know my boyfriend is a good guy, but I'm not gonna lie to him, and say he is everything!" Geneva replied.

Geneva had always been an early bloomer, and sometimes, Adina wished she had her daughter's unencumbered spirit. Now with Bella away, Geneva was the princess of the house. She no longer suffered the middle child syndrome, which had made her feel overpowered by Bella. She used to complain that being the middle child, she didn't get as much love as Bella or Haile. Adina, of course, had often taken those complaints seriously and tried to give a double dose of love to her second child, even when Geneva was only kidding.

Ten minutes later, Adina's cell phone rang. She thought it might be Haile's football coach, saying they had canceled his practice since it had started to snow as she was coming home. Outside, there was already a white powder covering the ground. The November temperatures in New York City had dropped, and the weather was definitely changing fast. Adina wasn't looking forward to another winter without a job. She took out her cell phone and saw that it said, "Unknown caller."

"Hello!" Adina answered at the second ring.

"Are you all right?" the caller asked. For a minute, Adina didn't recognize his voice.

"I'm fine, thank you," Adina said, clearing her throat when she realized it was Ben.

"In that case, I'm glad. Adina, I'm sorry; I know you went through a lot with everything that came into your life. But don't despair. There is always a light at the end of the tunnel, as they say."

Ben's words and tone had a calming effect upon Adina's ears. She still had mixed emotions about their meeting. At some level, she felt he had set a trap to meet her. On the other hand, she thought, it might have been a godly encounter.

"Thank you for saying that," she replied. "It means a lot to me. Not many people understand, but then, I don't tell those things to too many people anyway."

"But, you're planning to write a memoir. Those are the things you need to tell. It's your story, Adina! Don't deprive readers from learning from your life lessons. I really encourage you to open up, and tell it all. In the end, you'll feel empowered and nothing will ever bring you down again. Take it from my experience," Ben said.

"What do you mean? Did you write a memoir? I didn't know that! Why didn't you tell me?"

"Well, for starters, you weren't exactly in the mood, so I didn't have the courage," Ben said.

"Tell me now! What's your memoir's title? Please tell me!" Adina insisted.

"I have a feeling you will know before the end of the day. Just a hint: there are some juicy details about my life you might want to know before our Saturday date!"

Ben laughed out loud. Adina wasn't sure she wanted to know what juicy details he was talking about. But a surge to read his memoir became too strong for her to resist.

Before they hung up, Ben said, "By the way, I would like you to submit your short stories in the meantime. I'll refer you to a good editor to work with."

He said that publishing her short stories would help her to gain exposure, and it would also be a source of income supplement for Adina. She didn't tell Ben that it would actually be her only income at that point since, there was nothing much to supplement. The child support Charles paid was very minimal, considering the cost of life in New York City. But she was grateful that her ex-husband had agreed to help out with more of the kids' expenses.

After Adina hung up with Ben, she called Aleah to share the news of her new encounter—and the stinking fear she felt, mixed with excitement. Aleah was encouraging, and told her to lighten up on her "ridiculous standards."

"It's only a date, Adina, not a wedding!" Aleah was quick to remind her.

Around 7 p.m. that evening, the doorbell rang. It was Coach Barry bringing Haile home from football practice. Coach Barry was a retired firefighter, who had been a football player in college before he got injured, and had to let go of his dream of becoming an NFL player. He now coached school teams from elementary to high school on the island. For Barry, coaching those kids, and seeing some of them grow up to become football players themselves, was his passion. He was the kindest man Adina knew. After her divorce, she had wanted to withdraw Haile from his football team because money was tight. The membership fees and the additional football gear became too much of an expense for her. But, Coach Barry had refused to let Adina take Haile out of the junior league team. When she explained her reasons, Barry insisted he would pay for Haile's membership fees and uniform gear.

"Listen, Haile is like the grandson I never had. Please, let me help," Barry had said.

But Adina had absolutely refused to take his charity, so out of pride, she used her credit card to pay the fees.

"Then at least let me take him to his practices on Tuesdays, and you can bring him on Saturdays," Coach Barry had offered.

"But...." Adina didn't want to take advantage of Barry's kindness.

"No buts. I'm bringing the boy to practices on Tuesdays, and that's that!" Coach Barry had insisted.

Adina had given in then. Barry and his wife, Martha, were good friends to Adina. Since they lived in the same building, Martha was always bringing over treats for her kids. She and Barry had moved from Ireland as young adults, and now, their two grown children had moved back there where their extended family was; Barry and Martha rarely saw any of their relatives.

Since her kids didn't have a close relationship with their one remaining grandparent, Adina was grateful to have Barry and his wife Martha in her life. They shared Thanksgiving dinners in Adina's apartment, or they invited her and the kids to theirs. They were sorry she was alone with the kids after the divorce, but they had never liked Charles. They knew he was selfish, and had only hurt Adina more than he had helped her.

"Come in, sweetie; how was practice?" Adina asked when she opened the door to Haile and Barry.

"Mom, we won! We beat the Giants so badly!" Haile exclaimed, full of energy.

Adina offered Barry something to drink, but he declined. She thanked him for giving Haile a ride.

"Don't forget this Saturday is game day. Don't be late!" Coach Barry reminded Adina before going to his own apartment.

The kids were due to see their father that weekend, and she would also have her first date with Ben, so she hoped Charles would keep his word, and come to the game as he had promised her. It was so important for Haile to be encouraged by both his parents.

On Saturday, Adina planned to bring Haile to the game and have Charles take his son after. Geneva was invited to her friend's birthday and a sleepover that Saturday, and she would leave around 2 p.m. After each child was at his or her respective event, Adina would have time to get ready for Ben to take her out.

For the first time in a long time, Adina had something to look forward to. Her marriage to Charles had left her scarred, and distrustful of men. Ben was the first man she was trusting to take her on a real date, and he hadn't said kids were a deal breaker. She felt butterflies in her stomach as she thought about him. Adina wondered whether she might be falling for him as well, but she barely knew him. Loneliness could do strange things to people!

She decided she would go easy on herself and him, and see where their adventure would take them.

CHAPTER 10

It was a Friday night, during spring break, when Adina decided to share the good news with her kids. She had been seeing Ben for five months, so, she didn't want things to get too serious before she had her kids' blessing. So, she asked them to sit in the living room. It was March, and Bella had come home for spring break. As soon as Adina told the kids she was seeing Ben Neman, a former literary agent, now turned publisher, Bella responded with extreme anger.

"You only care about yourself! What about us?" Bella demanded in a shaking voice. She looked like she could slap her mother, she was so angry.

Bella's reaction surprised her mother. Adina had assumed her oldest daughter would be happy to hear she was in a relationship. Instead, Bella reacted negatively. She was totally against her mother being with a man other than her father, and she expressed raw emotions Adina never knew Bella could have. Suddenly, she treated her mother like her enemy and the cause of all her sufferings.

Bella had always been the grownup daughter in her mother's eyes. She was more reserved, and she barely shared her own emotions and feelings with her mother, or anyone for that matter. In many instances, she was like Adina in the way she kept things bottled up inside. She had replaced her feelings with her school work, and she got excellent grades to show for the time she invested in her studies. Although Adina was happy that her daughter was successful in school, she also worried about her lack of a social life. She wanted Bella to have a normal and balanced life.

Bella had always been the one her mother confided in—more so than her other children, mainly because she thought Bella was mature enough to understand her feelings. That was true when the feelings were about Adina's childhood, or divorcing Bella's father, or even the lack of datable men. Therefore, Adina hadn't thought it would cause any problem for Bella, if she started dating.

Geneva already knew about Adina's relationship with Ben, despite her mother's trying to hide it. She had suspected it long ago, although she had decided to keep quiet. She was just happy for her. She knew it was good for her mother to date again. She could see Adina looked happier, and more relaxed, since she and Ben had started dating. However, Geneva felt too intimidated by her older sister to speak up when Bella barked against their mother's dating news.

Before Adina could even respond to her oldest daughter's outrage, Bella stormed out of the living room, and went to her bedroom, slamming the door as she closed it.

Seeing her mother's chagrin, Geneva hugged her. She knew how lonely their mother had been before Ben. Bella lived at the campus dorm, so, she was not the one who had to hear their mother crying at night.

"Don't worry, Mom," Geneva said. "Bella will come around. Just give her some time. I think she needs a boyfriend of her own!"

Adina's smile was bittersweet. She really hoped so because she liked Ben a lot, and she thought he could be the one to bring into her kids' lives.

Then, she turned toward Haile to see how he was reacting.

"What about you? Do you hate me too?" Adina asked her son.

Haile just looked quietly at his mother with his big brown eyes, walked up to her, and gave her a bear hug.

"No, I love you, Mom. You're the best mom in the whole wide world!" Adina was touched by his words. She kissed him on his forehead and sent him to bed.

Haile didn't really care if his mother dated as long as she was happy. Deep down, he resented his father for all he had put their mother through. Even at his young age, he understood more than his mother credited him for. So, as far as Haile was concerned, another man was welcome, but he hadn't expressed that in front of Bella to avoid suffering his oldest sister's wrath. He thought girls acted weird sometimes. But it wasn't his place to say anything to them on this matter. He left it up to his sisters to have their own opinions on whether or not their mother should date.

The next day, Saturday, Adina was very distraught when she called Ben.

"Ben," she said, fearing how he would react, "I don't think we can continue to see each other."

"What happened?" Ben had known she was going to tell her children about them, and that she feared the reaction might be negative.

"The kids think," Adina sighed, "or at least Bella thinks, that I'm being selfish by indulging in romance."

"It's a normal reaction, Adina. Give it time; they will come around," Ben said trying to appease her anxiety. But, he had also heard stories where the kids wanted to dictate their parents' lives. Still, he tried to be positive as he added, "Teens have a tendency to be self-centered, but they eventually outgrow it."

"But Bella is not a teen anymore," Adina said. "She's an adult, and honestly, I thought she would be the one to be more supportive. But instead, she's putting into her siblings' heads all these negative ideas about me being with a man other than their father." Adina sounded depressed about it; she needed her oldest daughter's approval so much.

"Would you like me to talk to her?" Ben asked.

"To who? Bella? Ben, you're the last person she would want to talk to."

"You might be surprised. I have hidden talents that you don't know about!" Ben was trying to lighten up the conversation, but he was serious about talking to Bella. Adina was unsure whether it would help or just hurt more, but she trusted Ben, so she agreed.

"Alright, be my guest! When do you want to meet her? Her spring break ends next Sunday."

"I'll come over today, and take the four of you to dinner in Manhattan. I know the right place. I'll be there at six," Ben said, and then they hung up.

. . . .

When Ben showed up that evening, he had a bouquet of red roses for Adina and a box of pralines for the kids. He rang the doorbell, and Haile flew to the door to open it.

"Hi!" Haile said, as he gave a once over to the 6' 5" man.

"Hello! You must be Haile? Ben Neman!" Ben said as he shook Haile's hand. The two took each other's measurements and liked what they saw.

Ben could see Haile was a sweet boy, quick and sharp. Haile saw in Ben someone he could bounce ball with at the football field. But, he decided he was probably into baseball, or even tennis. Oh, man, he hoped Ben wasn't into tennis because, in Haile's mind, tennis was a girl's sport. But whatever sport, he already approved of his mother going out with Ben. As Ben came into the living room, Bella was watching television. She ignored him completely.

"Hi! You must be Bella! I'm Ben Neman," Ben said, extending his long hand to shake Bella's.

"I'm not deaf. I heard you," Bella lashed out without offering an inch of her hand.

Geneva now came out of her room. She had a little too much makeup on, but she was all smiles when she greeted Ben. *At least two out of three don't want to murder me; there is hope,* Ben thought.

When Adina appeared out of her bedroom, she looked stunning. Both Ben and Adina smiled at each other tenderly as they kissed, which disgusted Bella even more. She stood up and went to her room to get ready. She could feel that she had already lost the battle. She actually thought Ben and her mother looked good together. She could see her mother was happier in Ben's company. Adina had lit up when she saw him. Bella hadn't missed any detail, even though she had tried to appear disgusted by her mother's date. She also knew Haile would benefit from a male role model, since their father had missed every chance to be a father in the last twenty years.

Yes, Charles was coming around, but it was too late for Bella to benefit from her father's presence. She was now away in college, and she would soon graduate and move on with her life. It always put a sting in Bella's spirit whenever she thought about how she had missed her father's love and affection. She loved him so much, and she had idolized him for so long; hoping he would get his act together sooner, and be the father she and her siblings needed. When that didn't happen, Bella had accepted it, and she resorted to suppressing her pain with school work. She had never had a boyfriend; she thought she should wait to finish school first, then date, and get married. She wanted to have kids one day, and a family of her own to care for; that would make up for the missed affection from her father in her childhood. In many ways, she was like her mother, who had until now only dated one man, and married hastily so she could have a family to replace the one she had lost.

On the way to the restaurant, the kids talked animatedly; even Bella's anger had subsided. It had been a long time since the kids had seen a sense of wholeness in their mother's life, and in return, in their own lives. Ben was respectful, attentive, and fun to be with. He didn't force his opinions, but he listened with full intent. He asked the kids the right questions and wanted to get to know them.

Before they got to the restaurant, Bella said to her mother, "I'm sorry, Mom. I was a brat earlier, and I want to apologize to Mr. Neman."

"It's okay, sweetheart," said Adina. "We understand your reaction; and it's very normal. You expressed your true feelings, and that's what any good person does. Suppressing your emotions doesn't do anyone any good. So thank you, sweetie; I love you. I love all of you, and no one can ever take that away from you. Okay?"

Bella nodded her head in acceptance and the two hugged tightly.

Adina was happy to see that her kids relaxed after Bella's apology. They were now all on the same page, and it felt good. During the meal, they all chatted and laughed about different topics. Ben told them stories of his childhood in Israel, before his parents immigrated to the States forty-five years ago. They had lived in the Israeli settlements in East Jerusalem. But, due to political unrest, his parents, his sister, and he had fled to the United States of America when he was six. His father had been a successful businessman in Israel, but he had lost everything when he decided that the safety of his family was worth more than the money he was making.

Ben Sr. had sold his business to a government contractor, and come to New York with his wife and kids. They had bought a house on Long Island where he had started from scratch, in his garage, to build his literary agency. Twenty-five years later, the agency became one of the biggest and most successful in the country. When Ben's father had retired, he had asked him to take over. And until Ben had left the agency; it had remained one of the most successful literary agencies in the United States.

Ben had been committed to his career, and it was the reason why his two marriages had both been brief. But now, he wanted to settle down at age fifty-one and have a family. After his second marriage, he had never met the right woman, despite his dating efforts. Women always threw themselves at him, because he had money and charm, and he always ended up in a bit of a complicated situation, when the women began pressing for marriage proposals. But, now, Ben was happy that he had met Adina. She seemed to have come into his life through the grace of God. Before meeting Adina, he had given up on dating.

"Women these days, they want to be the man and the woman all at the same time." That was Ben's all-time complaint.

But his oldest sister always told him, "No, that only means you haven't met the right one, little brother…. And when you do, your own standards will go up in smoke."

"I sure do hope so because I'm getting tired…." Ben would add.

After meeting Adina, Ben felt like he had found the missing piece of himself. He felt peaceful and whole. He didn't need to try as hard as he had done with the other women he had dated in the past. He truly felt that with Adina, he could be himself, and that he might have finally found the one.

CHAPTER 11

At Geneva's high school graduation a few months later, Adina invited Ben, as well as Coach Barry and his wife Martha, and all of her best friend Aleah's family. Adina looked forward to the opportunity to introduce Ben to her friends. And when they all met in the auditorium a few minutes before the ceremony began, Aleah pulled Adina aside to let her know she was more than impressed with her choice of man!

"Girl, he's sexy. Mhh…Mhh…Mhhm! Nice fishing job, girlfriend. You outdid yourself this time!" Aleah said, clacking her tongue. Although she had already heard about Ben from Adina, Aleah hadn't had a chance to meet him in person. And until now, she hadn't thought it would be serious. She had given up on Adina when it came to romance.

Adina laughed, happy that her best friend approved of her choice of a man. Meanwhile, Aleah's husband, James, was chatting with Ben, and telling him how he had known Adina since she had lost her adoptive parents, and how much she had been through. He told Ben about Adina's marriage to Charles, and what a jerk the man had turned out to be.

"I hope you're the one for her, man! She could use a break and be happy for once. She and her kids deserve more than life has thrown at them," James said, subtly warning Ben not to play with Adina's heart. Adina was his wife's best friend, and they had all come to love her and her kids, as part of their own family, so James felt a little protective of her.

"I love her, man!" Ben said to appease James's worries. "She's the best thing that's ever happened to me. I'm fifty-one, not thirty, so I don't think I'm at the playing stage anymore. You have nothing to worry about. I want to be with her for the rest of my life. Despite what happened to Adina, she's resilient and a strong woman, and I love that about her."

They then entered the big auditorium and found seats together. The ceremony was about to begin, and the large audience started to clap as the graduates filed into the room. Parents snapped pictures, and some even recorded the speeches. Finally, the principal stood up to give his graduation speech.

"Dear students, today you have graduated from high school. And from now going forward, you have become adults. Thanks to your parents and your school body, you have grown wings, and now you will have to use them to fly out of the nest. You'll be responsible for your own mistakes, and sorry, your parents may not bail you out!"

Everyone laughed, and students high-fived each other. They were amused by the principal's speech. But they also knew he was giving them some food for thought.

As the principal continued his commencement speech, Adina had a flashback to her own high school graduation. Her adoptive parents had gone out of their way to make her day special. They had invited their friends and family to see the little girl they had saved from the Ethiopian orphanage become an adult, and fly on her own wings. She missed them so much, and tears welled up as she sat there, lost in her past. She couldn't help thinking about who her biological parents might have been. It was both a sorrow and a mystery to her, not knowing whom she came from. She didn't know whom she looked like more—her father or mother, or both? No one could tell her. She only knew her biological mother had had her at sixteen years old, and had died in childbirth. She never knew who her biological father was. That information hadn't been available at the orphanage, when Shelly and Mitch had adopted her. Maybe if she had lived, her mother would have shared with Adina who the father had been. Adina's biological mother Abeba, had gone to her grave with the secret of the man who had impregnated her.

As Adina got lost in her thoughts, thinking what kind of parents had engendered her, she envisioned two teenagers having wild sex in the fields of Ethiopia's countryside without inhibition. They had probably loved each other passionately, like any sixteen year old who idealizes love. She had a smile on her face as she thought about it. Then, Bella startled her out of her reverie.

"Mom, what's funny? You're smiling!"

"Oh, nothing, sweetie; I was just thinking." She dismissed her daughter's question and returned to the present and her second daughter's graduation.

• • • •

Two weeks after Geneva's graduation, Ben took Adina on a weekend getaway to Vermont, where he had reserved a room in a luxurious inn. The June weather was as wonderful as could be with luscious green all over the hills where the hotel was located. They drove all around small towns, and had dinner in a small Italian diner. When they went to their hotel, it was 7 p.m., and the sun still shone outside, but, they were a bit tired. They wanted to go to sleep early so they could do some more sightseeing before they left the next day. After they slipped into their hotel bathrobes and Adina turned on the TV, Ben opened the small fridge they had in the room, and took out a bottle of champagne.

"Wow! Champagne. What are we celebrating?" Adina asked.

"'What are we not celebrating?' should be the question, my dear!" Ben responded.

He took two glasses and poured champagne in both. He handed one to Adina. Then, while holding his glass in one hand, he knelt in front of her, dipped his hand in his pocket, and took out a small box. He then put his glass on the coffee table beside him, and said, "Adina, I love you with all my heart. I don't know what I would become without you; I want to spend the rest of my life with you. Will you marry me?"

Adina, who had been watching his every move, was astounded. When he opened the box to show her the ring, she burst out and cried for what seemed an eternity. She couldn't speak; she was in shock.

"It's really simple. Yes or No?" Ben said as he awaited her answer.

"Yes, yes…a gazillion yeses…" Adina finally said between sobs and sniffling.

Ben stood up and kissed her until she was almost out of breath.

"Cheers, my darling! I've waited for you for so long. Welcome home, baby!" Ben said as they sipped the champagne. They took their second sip of champagne, and then Ben set his glass on the coffee table again. He put his hand in hers and signaled her to stand up. He took her in his arms, embraced her, and kissed her ever so tenderly. Then he picked her up, and laid her on the bed, where they made passionate love for the first time.

"That was…wow!" Ben finally said.

It was past nine o'clock, and they had made love twice, but neither felt satiated.

"Can we do it again?" he asked her with a grin.

"Again? Tomorrow. Let's get some sleep," Adina said, giggling, which aroused him even more.

"But it's already tomorrow in China!" Ben objected.

They both laughed, and before they knew it, they were entangled under the sheets for another round of lovemaking. And right after, they both drifted off to sleep, and all was well in their world.

CHAPTER 12

Adina and Ben set their wedding date to coincide with Adina's birthday in August, when she turned forty-five. It was two months after their engagement. Adina had never liked to celebrate her birthdays, and she told Ben so. He chose that they would get married on her birthday, so their wedding anniversary would serve as a reminder to celebrate both her birthday and their anniversary.

They decided to have a medium-size wedding, mostly attended by Ben's family from Long Island and Adina's few friends from Maryland, Washington, D.C., Virginia, New York, and New Jersey. Adina sent out invitations, including one to her ex-husband Charles since they were now civil to one another, and even becoming friends. Adina didn't expect him to come to the wedding, but she thought an invitation would be a form of peace offering. Charles declined the invitation, but he sent her a gift in advance. Definitely, Charles was being born again, both literally and figuratively. He was now attending an

Episcopal church in Brooklyn, and started getting involved in many social justice activities there. When Adina received his gift, she decided to call Charles to thank him.

"Thank you for the gift," she told him. "Take care of yourself, Charles. Just so you know, I don't hate you anymore. And for what it's worth, I loved you, and our children will always be the tie that binds us."

"I loved you too, Adina," he replied, "and I always will. You deserve to be happy, and you deserve someone who treats you better than I did or could. I'm sorry we couldn't make it work, but I'm sure there is a reason God brought us together."

Charles grew pensive as he continued.

"I read somewhere that, sometimes, soulmates mean two souls mating so they can do the work in their evolving. And when that happens, each soul is free to go on its own journey and to keep expanding. I think that's what happened with us, Adina."

"So," Adina replied, "you mean, or whatever you read means we were both hurting, and the purpose of our marriage was to bring our baggage to the surface, so we could heal?"

"That's exactly it!" Charles confirmed. "I came into your life to help you—well, more like to cause you pain that was similar to what you had gone through—your abandonment issues, for instance, so you could face it, reflect on it, and eventually, heal your wounded heart."

Then Charles admitted the source of his sudden wisdom.

"Actually, to be honest, I've been seeing a psychotherapist. She helped me understand myself more than I had ever cared to."

"Okay! And according to your psychotherapist, I came into your life to achieve...what exactly?" Adina hesitantly asked. She wasn't sure she wanted to know. But, if this therapy thing could help either of them heal from their respective wounded pasts, then she was willing to continue this conversation.

"Well, Dr. Beckman thinks that your part in my life was to remind me of my father. Ha-ha.... Remember when I used to tell you that you sounded like my father?"

Yes, she remembered, and it used to hurt like a sharp knife in her soul.

"How could I forget? It was your signature statement whenever we had an argument. And I might have taken it as a compliment, if you didn't always say it while I was hurting!" Adina reminded him.

"I'm truly sorry, Adina. I was a mess and in a rage. I couldn't control my emotions whenever I thought about my father. And anyone who said anything similar to what he used to say to me, became my enemy."

Now that his father was dead, Charles regretted the time he had spent being angry at him and missing out on his dad's love because of his pride, hatred of authority, and foolishness.

"I'm sorry, too, that it didn't work out between us," said Adina. "But, I know the right woman will come into your life when you're ready for her. Just keep expanding your soul, and keep your heart open for the right one to enter."

Adina wished her ex-husband well, and they hung up.

After their phone call, they both felt free. Adina smiled, as she thought again of their souls having come together to mingle, so they could heal their pasts. What a smart life philosophy that was! She was impressed by whoever had discovered it.

Now, Adina was ready to enter Ben's soul. She felt certain his had already gone through the transformational stage. She had no fear in marrying Ben like she had felt when she married Charles. Everything with Charles had been a struggle from the very first day, but she had kept strong for the marriage to survive, until it couldn't.

Some souls just weren't meant to stay together after their work was done. She understood that now. And she was happy to enter this new stage of her life, and find the happiness and security of heart she had been seeking for so long.

CHAPTER 13

As Adina walked down the aisle on Berhanu's arm for the second time, in the small church in the Williamsburg neighborhood in Brooklynn, she couldn't contain her tears. But this time, they were tears of joy. She felt like she had come home when Berhanu presented her to Ben, and she had no creeping doubts like she had experienced the day she married Charles Kumi. She totally felt in sync with Ben, and she knew when he held her hand as they walked up the church aisle, that she had made the right decision.

Aleah was Adina's matron of honor for the second time, and she couldn't have been any happier for her best friend to have finally found a good man. The kids were all there—Bella and Geneva were their mother's bridesmaids in matching dresses, and Haile, in his cute tux, was the ring bearer— a job he took very seriously. The kids had long accepted Ben as a part of the family, and they loved his paternal presence, which they had missed out on while growing up with an absentee father.

Ben was good to the kids. He played basketball with Haile and tennis with the girls. Haile accepted the fact that Ben didn't play football, and had converted to liking basketball. Haile was in the sports exploration phase, and for him, what mattered wasn't the sport he played, but whom he played with. Playing basketball with Ben was an added incentive for Haile to like the sport.

For two weeks, Adina and Ben honeymooned in Italy, visiting Rome, Venice, and Florence; then they went to Barcelona for another week. It was a wonderful trip, and Adina enjoyed every minute of it, since she had never gone anywhere while married to Charles. Before that, she had been to Paris, London, and Geneva with her adoptive parents, when they had attended international conferences, when she was a little girl in elementary school. She had told Ben when they were dating that her ultimate dream trip was to go to Ethiopia, but there had been no opportunity for her to do so. Lately, she had been learning the Amharic language, and often practiced with Berhanu's wife on the phone. She now knew how to say some words in Amharic such as *"Selam, endemin-neh?"* meaning, "Hello, how are you?"

The day Adina and Ben came back from their honeymoon, her book was released; and for six consecutive weeks, it became number one on *The New York Times'* bestseller list. Adina and Ben went on the book tour, before they had even unpacked from their honeymoon. He wanted to support her as much as possible. They toured the country, and had a blast, stopping at libraries and schools, and appearing on television and radio shows to talk about her new book. The story in Adina's memoir resonated with many people who had been adopted, as well as those who had adopted or wanted to in the future.

• • • •

One Saturday morning, almost three months after her wedding, Adina was making breakfast for Haile and Geneva. Ben had left early that morning to meet an agent to negotiate two new book deals for his publishing company. Adina had been in the kitchen cutting onions, green peppers, tomatoes, cilantro, and basil to make an omelet, when everything suddenly went dark, and she couldn't see anything.

Before she could reach for a chair in the dining room, she fainted and fell down buttocks first. Geneva was in the living room watching her favorite TV show. Haile was out of the house, playing with his next-door friend. Geneva heard a big boom, and when she turned to look at her mother, Adina was lying on the floor. Geneva ran to her mother, and started to scream, which woke her up.

"Mom, are you okay? What happened?" Geneva asked with frightened eyes.

Adina didn't understand what had just happened to her. She asked Geneva to help her stand up. Then, once on her feet again, she said, "I don't know, sweetheart; how long was I on the floor?"

As Adina stood up, she couldn't stand the smell of the omelet she was making. She gagged several times, and had to go to the bathroom where she threw up. Her stomach hurt, she felt lightheaded, and she asked Geneva to bring her a glass of water.

"Mom, are you pregnant?" Geneva asked.

"Don't be silly—at my age? And it's inappropriate for you to ask those kinds of questions."

Adina tried to dismiss her daughter's question, but she couldn't help thinking, *Oh, my God! Is it still possible?* She remembered the same sickness had happened when she had gotten pregnant with Haile. But now, at forty-five, going on forty-six, she didn't think that chapter was still possible in her life. And as she thought about it, she became aware that she hadn't had her period for the last two months, which she had thought was probably the start of a pre-menopausal phase.

"Are you serious? Mom, I'm not four!" Geneva reminded her. "Just call your man, and tell him we're having a baby! I hope it's a girl…*cause* I don't want another Haile pestering me."

Geneva was clearly ahead of her mother who was still in denial that she could get pregnant at her age. She and Ben hadn't been using any protection since they got married; she had never taken birth control pills in her life, and she didn't intend to start at her age.

"Oh, my God, what if I'm actually pregnant?" she blurted out. "But it can't be possible!"

"Mom, you're only forty-five, not sixty-five! I've heard that many women are having babies at an older age now. Many actresses have babies in their forties and even fifties now, Mom!" Geneva told her mother in a tutoring tone.

Thirty minutes later, Ben came back home, just in time for lunch and hopefully a *quickie* before he went back to meet another agent for a book deal prospect. When he saw his stepdaughter was home, however, he instantly knew the quickie wasn't going to happen. *Oh, well!* Ben thought to himself.

By then, Adina had already taken a pregnancy test with a kit she bought at a CVS pharmacy, just down the street. And yes, the test was positive! She was pregnant. She had mixed feelings about it. Was she ready to go through another pregnancy and raise another baby again? She thought she had been there and done that already. With Ben, it was time for her to enjoy her life and see her children grow up, and go out into the world. She felt that she and Charles had been blessed with three beautiful and healthy children, and she didn't need anymore kids.

It wasn't like Ben wanted children or anything. He had never mentioned it to her, and he seemed to enjoy helping his wife raise hers from her first marriage. On the other hand, happy thoughts flooded Adina's mind, as she played with the idea of having Ben's baby. She felt excitement just thinking how this child would be born into a loving relationship, and grow up in a loving home with two attentive and affectionate parents.

In her first marriage, Adina had struggled being a sole parent to her kids, while Charles chased *bimbos*, and drank uncontrollably.

"Hi Geneva, what's up? Where is your mother?" Ben asked as he hugged his stepdaughter Geneva in the living room. Then, he went to the fridge to get a bottle of water. Meanwhile, Adina had been in the bathroom, throwing up for the second time since her fainting. Then, Geneva saw her time alone with Ben in the living room, as an opportunity to test his knowledge of biology.

"Hi, Ben!" she said. "At what age do you think a woman stops having kids?"

"Um…thirty-nine?" Ben answered.

It sounded like a trick question, but Ben didn't give it a second thought.

"Wrong! Even in their fifties, women can still conceive. That's what happened to Grandma. She had my dad in her fifties," Geneva informed Ben.

Ben just shrugged his shoulders, and took a sip from his water bottle.

But, Geneva continued, "With my mom, you have nothing to worry about. She's still pretty young, right?"

Ben was always amused by Geneva's discussions. He liked the way she expressed herself, and that she wasn't shy or afraid to challenge him sometimes with interesting topics. He smiled and went into his home office to check whether he had any phone messages.

When Adina came out of the bathroom, Ben was in their bedroom taking his work shirt off, so he wouldn't mess it up while eating lunch. Adina gave him a suspicious smile, as he pulled her to the bed, and planted a hard kiss on her lips.

"Wow, Mister, careful! Mama Bear here is very fragile," Adina said as Ben sat on the edge of their bed.

"Fragile? What that's supposed to mean? I knew you were a virgin when I married you, so, I've been very gentle," Ben teased her.

"Oh, yeah? But not so gentle because you injected a little head that's now growing inside of me."

Adina's words made Ben sit up straight. She had had time to meditate on what to say to her husband before he came home; and having his child felt right to her. She only hoped it would be the same for her husband. She wasn't sure where he stood on the whole baby thing, since they had never given it a thought. They had both assumed they were too old to have a baby. They were just enjoying their life together, while raising Adina's children from her previous marriage. And for Ben, inheriting three beautiful children with a woman he adored was a pretty good deal.

"What did you just say?" Ben asked with wide-open eyes.

"Aaah…, don't freak out! I already have kids. If anyone should freak out, it should be me." Adina said and she chuckled. As a matter of fact, she could see Ben was freaking out.

"Oh, my God, you're pregnant, are you?" said an overjoyed Ben. "Why didn't you tell me? When did you find out?"

"Honey, I can only answer one question at a time. And yes, I'm pregnant, and it's yours by the way in case you were wondering. And I just found out today, while making an omelet that almost killed me. All of a sudden, the eggs' odor made me sick, and I fainted. I'm lucky Geneva was home to help me." Ben continued to stare at his wife, while Adina added, "And I have no idea how old this thing is. All I know is that I missed my period for the last two months, and I thought I had hit menopause."

Ben took Adina in his embrace and held her sooo tightly.

"Thank you, sweetheart; you have no idea how happy I am right now," Ben said as tears started filling his eyes.

Adina had never seen this side of Ben—his mushy and sentimental side. When Ben went back to his office that afternoon, he was in a state of elation, and he shared the good news with his partners and friends at work, and anyone who cared to listen to his announcement.

At his age, Ben had thought that this blessing in the form of a baby was out of his reach. He never had kids with any of his previous wives. They were from the modeling world, and didn't want to ruin their figures having babies, and had told him so. He just didn't understand why he had been drawn to such women in the first place.

Ben had just turned fifty-two, and when the baby would be born, he would be close to fifty-three. But, he was finally going to be a father; he now had an offspring to carry on his name and legacy. He had thought that at Adina's age, it was quasi-impossible to have kids, but he loved her for who she was and didn't mind. If he had wanted to marry only to have children, there were lots of twenty-five to thirty-five year olds he could have married. But, he wanted someone he loved, and that someone happened to be Adina who was now forty-five.

Ben was happy just to be a stepfather to his wife's three kids, and to give them a life their own father had denied them. He was everything Charles had never been. He was fun-loving, caring, affectionate, attentive, and appreciative. In many ways, he reminded Adina of her adoptive dad, Mitch Springfield, now gone forever. Adina was everything to Ben, and she was as loving and affectionate to him. They brought out the best in each other.

All Ben's friends who were his age had college age kids, and he had settled with the idea that it was too late, until now. Nothing could have made him happier. And it was even more meaningful for him to create a family with Adina, an Ethiopian orphan whose life had not been easy. He was grateful he was a part of what gave her closure on her past experiences.

CHAPTER 14

Baby Azarel Mitch Neman came into the world in May. Adina and Ben named him Azarel, which meant "with the assistance of God" in Hebrew, and was fitting for their circumstances. His middle name, Mitch, was after Adina's adoptive father, Mitch Springfield. Azarel was a bundle of joy for the whole family, and he was particularly appreciated by Haile, who was happy to have another boy in the house. He liked to see himself as the big brother, the protector against the wrath of girls, which he had experienced from his sisters. The girls were just as happy. The kids all loved Azarel so much; they constantly took turns picking him up and carrying him around.

When the baby was two months old, Ben decided to leave Manhattan and move the family to New Jersey, to a bigger house where it was quieter than in New York City. He started working more from home, and he did most of his meetings via Skype. He only went to the city to meet important clients and attend key company meetings. Ben wanted to be there for Adina and help her with the baby, especially, when the other kids were away at school. And he said he didn't want to miss any step in his son's development. He wanted to be there when the baby would roll onto his tummy, stand in his crib, or take his first step. And he made sure he recorded every moment in Azarel's life.

Baby Azarel's baptism was held on his first birthday. Despite his Jewish upbringing, Ben did not practice the Jewish religion. Before he met Adina, he didn't really go to any church. But now, he had apparently been converted, and he didn't mind raising his son as a Christian.

They invited only close family and friends, and the baptism was held in a small church in Morris Township, New Jersey. After the church service, they went home for a reception in their backyard, where Ben barbecued. The weather was cooperative, and everyone who came felt a sense of bliss. Baby Azarel, who had started walking at eleven months, was now running everywhere, touching and bringing down everything in his reach. He giggled and enjoyed his christening day. In addition to the meat Ben barbecued, Adina had ordered platters of sandwiches, vegetable trays, and a huge cake. Everybody who mattered in Adina's life was there, from Virginia, Maryland, and Washington, D.C. Ben's parents had come from Miami, where they had retired. His oldest sister, who still lived in Israel, had come as well with her son. Other guests were

Ben's closest friends and some of his business partners in the publishing industry. It was a beautiful, pleasant day, and both Adina and Ben glowed with joy.

Adina had invited Charles at Ben's request. He believed in family and was close to his own parents. He was sorry for his stepkids because their father had not been very present in their lives, although Charles had started making an effort in recent years. For his stepchildren's sake, Ben tolerated Charles, and asked Adina to invite him to their son's christening. Ben couldn't understand how one could miss out on God's most precious gifts given through children. He had told Adina that he had learned so much from her children, more than he was teaching them. They brought him immense joy and many insights on life.

When Charles came to Adina and Ben's house that day, he wasn't alone. He was accompanied by a man who looked to be in his early forties. He had a light brown skin, was a bit taller than Adina, and was very handsome. When Adina first saw him entering her house, she felt sharp sensations in her body, feelings she couldn't identify. As she took another glance at him, a weird thing happened; she saw herself. He looked like someone she had seen in the past, but as she scanned her mind, she couldn't remember where.

As he shook Adina's hand, he introduced himself as Tengene Gesse. Adina almost collapsed. His name was

Ethiopian! Of that much, she was sure. But, what she wasn't sure of, was why in the world this man was with Charles; and what was he doing in her house?

At first, Adina thought he might be Berhanu's friend or relative. But, Berhanu had never mentioned him to Adina when they spoke on the phone. He had called her to excuse himself for not coming to Baby Azarel's christening, because he and his wife had moved to Seattle to be close to their son who lived there. Seattle was too far away for them to travel to the East Coast often.

Adina swallowed a gallon of her saliva to keep her emotions down; then she extended her hand to the stranger and said, *"Tena yistilign,"* which meant "Hello" in Amharic. Her heart was pounding so hard that she was sure all the guests could hear it. Her breast milk started to overflow. She could feel it welling up, and then pouring down her stomach under her nursing bra. She had to excuse herself and go to her bedroom to place a nursing pad under her bra. She quickly changed her shirt, and put on a different skirt. Then she ran to the refrigerator, poured herself a big glass of cold water, and took a long quenching sip.

Adina didn't know who the Ethiopian man was, but deep down, in her heart of hearts for some reason, she had a feeling she knew who he was. Her intuition was telling her who the man might be, but she kept fighting it. How was it possible? It couldn't be!

After she changed her clothes, Adina returned to the backyard where the guests were talking animatedly. She stood beside her husband, and Ben looked into her eyes with deep affection as he held her hand. He then guided her to where Charles and the stranger were standing.

"Adina, I believe you already met Mr. Tengene Gesse. Did Charles tell you he's the new Ethiopian Ambassador to the United Nations?"

Ben's tone told Adina there was more to the ambassador than met the eye. She needed to know before she went nuts. She nodded at Ben's words and softly replied, "No, I didn't know." Then she said, addressing Mr. Gesse, "That's wonderful! But, it must be hard being so far from home."

"Yes," said Mr. Gesse, "and I'm sorry if I crashed your party, but Mr. Kumi was kind enough to invite me, and I don't know many people in New York City yet."

Adina wasn't really listening; she was lost in her thoughts, analyzing him like a case study. Despite his strong accent, his English was fluent, and he was soft-spoken, self-confident, with an almost aristocratic air, mixed with a humbleness Adina had never seen before in people working in high-rank positions.

"Sweetheart!" Ben called Adina from her reverie. "The ambassador has something to tell you, but, I think we should probably wait until the other guests are gone."

"Of course, no problem." was all Adina could say.

She then returned inside the house to nurse the baby, who had awakened from his nap upstairs. Adina was glad the baby was awake, so she could nurse, because her breast milk couldn't stop overflowing.

Three hours later, everyone left except Charles and Mr. Gesse. They retreated to the living room, where it was more private. That's when Charles disclosed the secret he had been keeping from Adina.

"I found you a brother, Adina!" Charles blurted out.

Wide-eyed and not knowing how to reply, Adina waited while Charles explained.

Charles told how one day, he was at a UN General Assembly, when he met the new ambassador of Ethiopia to the United Nations who was attending the same meeting. Charles's work at the UN had always been related to African development, and he was involved in the research and statistics for the millennium development goals. He worked closely with heads of African nations and their ambassadors. After the meeting, Charles had walked into the ambassador's office and introduced himself.

"Mr. Gesse, I'm Charles Kumi. I met you at the UN Assembly this morning. I work in the Millennium

Development Goals department," Charles said as the two men firmly shook hands.

The ambassador showed Charles to a chair across from his, and they both sat down. As they talked about New York life among other things, Charles's eye spotted Adina's book sitting on Mr. Gesse's desk.

"May I?" Charles asked, as he took the book in his hands. Then, he asked Mr. Gesse, "Do you know who the author is?"

"Yes…I mean not in person!" said Mr. Gesse. "But I do hope to meet her one day."

"Well, I think I can arrange that!" Charles said, knowing his ex-wife would be thrilled to meet the Ethiopian ambassador. It was as if Charles knew both his ex-wife and the ambassador had something in common, though he just couldn't put his finger on it. But, he was planning to find out for Adina's sake.

"Did you enjoy reading her book?" Charles asked.

"I thought it was a masterpiece; Adina did a great job sharing her life story."

Charles himself had enjoyed reading Adina's book; especially, learning about the many things she had not shared with him during their marriage. He hadn't really been a good listener then. Adina had only shared with him slightly, without going into details, and she didn't know the whole story of her birth circumstances either.

But whatever she knew, Adina had never felt Charles was the right person to confide in about her innermost troubles that she carried from her childhood. Even what she had shared with him, he had used to insult her once they had started fighting.

When Charles read his ex-wife's book, he finally understood why she behaved the way she did, and why she kept to herself many of those details. They were things one only bears in one's heart, until one finds the right person to open up to. Charles had not been that person for Adina. He knew that much about himself now. He just thanked God for having brought Adina into his life to confront their past and, eventually, work on healing his own life as well. But Charles didn't regret their marriage anymore. He now knew there had been a purpose to their union, however long it had lasted. In addition, they had been blessed with three beautiful children for whom he was grateful, now that he was a born-again Christian. Before, he had rebelled against anyone who wanted to claim his responsibility.

"I found her book in the bookstore on 42nd Street when I first arrived in New York City," Mr. Gesse explained to Charles. "I think I was attracted by the author's Ethiopian name. Because, let's be honest, you don't have many Ethiopian authors in bookstores here, my brother! As soon as I finished the first chapter about her life, from birth to five years old, before she was adopted, I knew she was my sister."

"Hold on now Ambassador Gesse! Sister? I don't believe Adina had any sibling." Charles interjected. After all, he knew her better than the ambassador; he had been married to her for eighteen years. Even if he didn't know the many details of his ex-wife's early life, at least he knew she didn't have any brothers or sisters in Ethiopia, or anywhere else for that matter.

"Yes, I know, Mr. Kumi. Adina never had brothers or sisters she knew of. But that's the story here!" The ambassador continued as Charles listened intently.

Charles couldn't believe Adina had hidden that part of her life, too! Finally, he felt he and his ex-wife had lived together like strangers—not as a married couple with three kids together.

"You see," the ambassador started to explain, "her adoption took place when she was five years old. That's when she came to America, and that's probably the part she remembers best. In her early years, she mentions the circumstances of her birth mother, a teenage girl who was thrown out of high school when she got pregnant, right?"

But Charles had also read the book, and had learned those details. He still didn't know why this man claimed to be Adina's brother.

"What Adina doesn't know is that when her mother, Abeba, was a high school student, she went to live with her uncle, a man named Berhanu Lule. Mr. Lule worked for the Ethiopian government's foreign affairs. There, he worked under my father, who eventually became the Ambassador of Italy, and that's basically where I grew up, and attended Law School in Rome."

Charles was looking the ambassador in the eyes, not really understanding how he was Adina's brother. But he kept quiet and listened as Mr. Gesse continued.

"This is a part I'm not proud to talk about regarding my father. He has since passed away, but he made sure he told me the story, so I would look for Adina—Abeba's baby, and share it with her. My father wasn't proud of what he had done in his life, when it came to women, but this instance was the shame of his life."

Mr. Gesse continued, "One day, my father sent Mr. Lule to Sudan for a work assignment, and promised him he would look after his young niece Abeba, who was in high school and living with her uncle. The two men had always been good friends, so there was no doubt Mr. Lule trusted his boss, my father. That night, my father came to see Abeba, and he lost it. I mean he lost his mind! He slept with the girl. After that? Well…after that, the rest is history! Abeba was sixteen years old, and after the encounter with my father, she got pregnant and gave birth to Adina."

Charles's eyes opened wide as he listened to the ambassador tell a story of rape, and molestation as if it were a fairy tale. His fist formed as if he might punch the ambassador in the face, but he restrained himself and kept his cool. It was a good thing Charles no longer drank alcohol; he would have not kept his cool at all. Mr. Gesse didn't miss noticing how upsetting the story was for Charles, but, he continued.

"Mr. Kumi, I know this is the most shameful and horrible thing one can do to a girl. But when my father told me with tubes coming out of his nose on the hospital bed in Addis Ababa, he swore that he had not planned it. He claimed it was from too much whiskey he had consumed that night, and that his state of mind was blurred." The ambassador said as much as his father had cared to share with him before dying.

"I don't know about here in America, but in my culture," the ambassador continued, "as in many African cultures, when a girl gets pregnant, she is always the one blamed. I'm not proud of that, of course. But those are the cultural hindrances that need to be looked at and changed. Adina's mother was shunned, and unfortunately, she died giving birth to her. Adina's grandmother raised her in her toddler years, and then Adina was taken in by a distant cousin, when her grandmother died. Later, that cousin placed Adina in an orphanage in Addis Ababa, which was where she was when the American couple adopted her, and brought her to America."

Charles had been listening to the ambassador tell all the details he had not known in his ex-wife's story. Adina didn't know about the circumstances of her conception either, and she hadn't even wanted to look further into that part of her life. She just knew she had been born to a teenage mother who had died, and that she was adopted, and later came to the United States of America.

It was a lot to take in, even for Charles. He knew his ex-wife would eventually want to learn about these details, but he wasn't sure how she would react to this news brought by the ambassador of Ethiopia.

"So, basically, you're Adina's brother from another mother?" Charles finally said.

"Yes," said Mr. Gesse. "And I would like to tell Adina myself, because I promised my father on his deathbed that I would find Adina, and make things right, at least for her. She needs to know these things, and I want to be in her life if she lets me."

Charles then told Mr. Gesse about Adina and Ben's baby, and that he was getting baptized. They decided that it would be a good time for introducing the ambassador to Adina. Charles decided he wouldn't tell Adina he was bringing a guest; he didn't want to spoil the surprise. And he also knew how emotional anything related to Ethiopia made Adina feel. It seemed Charles cared more about Adina's feelings now that they were divorced, than when he was married to her.

"What happened between the two of you, by the way?" the ambassador now asked, turning the tables on Charles.

"Mr. Gesse, it's a story I'm not proud to tell anyone. It was my fault; I was a fool, and I did some things I'm not proud of myself. She is a wonderful woman, and a great mother to our three children. Her new husband, Ben Neman is lucky to have her." Charles replied, almost with regrets in his voice. But, he knew Adina had now moved on, and so, did he.

The ambassador saw the regrets in Charles's eyes, so he didn't want to press him for details. He was just happy his encounter with Charles would bring him to see his half-sister, the sister he had never been able to meet, until now.

CHAPTER 15

In Adina and Ben's living room, emotions were flying high. Adina discovered she had a brother she never knew about, but who knew everything about her early life; even how she was conceived.

Through him, she discovered who her biological mother was, and where she came from. She learned about her biological father whose indecent behaviors had cost him his career, when the government had finally learned that he had slept with Abeba. He had been an ambassador in Italy when the scandalous news broke. It was still a mystery how it got known, but Berhanu's houseboy made sure Abeba's memory would not be shunned unjustly forever.

It was the houseboy who had told someone in the Ethiopian government's secret service about how he had left Abeba home alone with the old man, who obviously didn't have any morals, and had slept with a child. What the houseboy didn't know was that the old man had actually raped Abeba, and not have consensual sex, as Boss had pretended it was, when he had told his son on his deathbed.

After the government learned of the incident, Berhanu's boss was called back to Ethiopia and fired from ever holding another government job. From there, his life went downhill, until his death. His son, Tengene Gesse, now himself an ambassador of Ethiopia to the United Nations, had studied political sciences and law in Rome, and mostly lived in Europe. When he had learned about his father's being ill, and on his deathbed, he had come home to see him. And that's when the old man had told his son all the details of the *girl's* life, as he referred to Abeba.

Boss had investigated on his own to find how Abeba's life had fared, after she left her uncle's house. He had known Abeba's uncle Berhanu had sent her back to her mother in Northern Ethiopia, when she got expelled from school because she was pregnant. Later, after Berhanu was no longer living in Ethiopia, Boss had learned about the child Abeba had given birth to, and that she had been adopted in America. He also knew Abeba had died in child birth. But, all this had remained a secret until Berhanu's houseboy told on Boss to the Ethiopian government secret service.

Before Boss died, he had asked his son to find out what had become of the child, Abeba gave birth to, no matter what it took; and to apologize to her on his behalf. The old man had committed a horrific act, and he did not want to go to his grave before having the chance to make it right. But he knew there was no way of making it right. The only way he could find solace was to find Adina, and he had been unable to achieve that. Thus, Boss had asked his son, Tengene Gesse, to find and apologize to Adina for their father's sins.

As Ambassador Gesse's story about Adina's past unraveled, Adina cried for a father and a mother she would never meet, but she was glad there was someone from her bloodline she could hold on to. She now had someone to call family in addition to the one she had created for herself, with the help of first Charles, and now Ben. Now, her extended family would include a brother, nephews and nieces, and a sister-in-law, and other family members she had never known existed until now.

The first thing Adina did after she learned she was related to Berhanu, was to call him. She was still shaken from all the information provided by the ambassador. But she did a good job of composing herself, so she could tell Berhanu what she had just learned. Berhanu's reaction surprised her. He told Adina he had suspected she was his great-niece from the very first day he had met her. But, when he had tried to ask her about her origins, she only told him about her American parents, not the circumstances of her birth, most of which she didn't know herself, until now.

After a long silence, Adina told Berhanu how his boss had molested and sexually violated her then sixteen-year-old mother, Abeba.

"I guess I'm the product of that shame," Adina said as fresh tears filled her eyes and her voice turned into broken, barely audible sounds. But this time, she wasn't alone in the world. In a way, she was crying with a mixture of emotions. She needed to release her past, embrace her joyful present and hope for a brighter future.

Now, Adina had her family, and Ben, her loving and caring husband. She had Berhanu, an uncle who had been treating her like family, without even knowing they were related. She had just found a half-brother with whom she shared blood and a past. And now, she would share the future. Even Charles had found his peace in knowing Adina, and they had three beautiful children together. Adina was no longer alone in the world.

After Adina finished talking with Berhanu, she sat down and wiped her tears. Ben sat beside her, and handed her another tissue to blow her nose.

"Sweetheart, are you all right?" he asked Adina. "This is a lot to take in. But, know that I'll always be here for you." Ben pulled her closer, kissed her, and hugged her tightly. Adina took a deep breath and smiled at her husband, as they embraced tenderly.

It had been an emotional life journey for Adina, one that she had lived with so much sorrow. But now, she had found so much joy in the end.

Adina's world seemed complete now. The pieces of the puzzle she had missed for so long were now found, and the puzzle solved. She felt she was home at last. Everyone toasted her family reunion, and with her hand locked into her newfound brother's, Adina announced that she wanted to go to Ethiopia the following year to visit the orphanage, where she had been placed before being adopted.

She had her newfound brother to thank for opening that door; a door to a world she had never thought would be hers again. She decided to start fundraisings for school supplies, books, clothing, toys, and medical equipment to bring to the orphanage. She also gave a handsome financial gift from her book proceeds to help build a new, fully-equipped orphanage. She wanted to give the orphans a place they could grow up, and aspire to a great future, despite their lots in life.

Adina also set out to advocate for the victims of sexual abuse, and to fight for the girls' education worldwide. This became her calling. From being an orphan to becoming a global voice for other orphans and girls, Adina wanted to give back to her global community, and to the orphans of Ethiopia. She was now in a place where she could afford to do that; both emotionally and financially.

Later that night, after everyone went to bed, Adina took out her journal and wrote:

"In the end, things work out the way they are supposed to. In the end, love conquers all and wins over evil. But, life is a duality of good and bad, and everything in between. How we respond to those events is what makes the difference in our lives. There are things we can change, but there are also things we cannot change. We need to acknowledge those things, and change what we can. And those we cannot change, we need to accept them, forgive ourselves, forgive others and let go. The life lessons we hope to learn on our journeys, often come from the adversities in our lives. The purpose of living is to allow our souls to evolve and transform the adversities in our lives into our calling."

Through it all, Adina concluded that life is always a little easier, when we have a listening ear, an understanding heart, and a **Hand to Hold**.

• • • •

THE END!

If you enjoyed
A HAND TO HOLD,

Here's a sneak peek at Seconde
Nimenya's inspiring memoir,

EVOLVING THROUGH ADVERSITY

Introduction

CONQUERING MY EMOTIONS

Anyone who survived childhood has enough material to write for the rest of his or her life.

— **Flannery O'Connor**

I first read the above quote in Anne Lamott's *Bird by Bird: Some Instructions on Writing and Life,* a book our writing instructor assigned us when I took my writing class. This passage struck me because I was feeling a little insecure about sharing my own childhood survival stories, but I decided that maybe— just maybe— my story was worth telling.

This book explores my life journey, my efforts to fit in, and the different guardian angels who have crossed my path along the way. It is not meant to teach politics or history. If I happen to talk about people, historical events or facts, it is to reminisce on those events because they impacted my life directly or indirectly in that time and place, and to the best of my recollection. Distances are an estimate in equivalent miles. I use real names when talking about my family members, but in some cases, I've changed or withheld names of some people to protect their privacy.

After reading this book, my hope is that you will feel uplifted. I intend it to carry a message of awareness, peace, nurturance, love, harmony, and forgiveness in our families, our communities, our countries, and our world. This is a story of breaking free from beliefs I no longer hold, and resilience by accepting and honoring who I am.

This story evolved from several emotional journals I have kept over the years. Sometimes, the emotional journals were my best friends where I could expose my feelings without shame or interruption. Some days, I would feel emotionally heavy and write something in my journal while my eyes would be blurred by tears. What I love about journaling your feelings is that you don't have to edit them for appropriateness. You just dive in with a pen, and pour your heart on the paper. It feels so good afterwards that you think, "What was I so sad about? Or why was I so angry?" Journaling your feelings gives you clarity, and you can make sound decisions after. It's a type of meditation (or even cheap therapy!) where you take a break and can make conscious choices afterward.

Journaling is a coping mechanism that can help you deal with whatever is at hand— whether it's a difficult decision you have to make or you just have to get the negative emotions out of your system, so no one gets hurt.

My intention is to inspire you to rise above your circumstances, whatever they may be, so you can thrive by discovering who you are and honoring your true self. Maybe life has given you lemons, but you didn't always know how to make lemonade. We all have things to battle in this life, some small, some big. And we all cope differently —some well, some not so well. Let's learn from each other.

Are you ready to begin honoring your true self? Can we take this life journey together? Do you have an open mind? I will hold your hand and you will hold mine; I want us to mentor each other and help each other grow. Don't spend another day living with a heavy load on your shoulders. Let's go to the school of life together.

Part 1: Africa

THE EARLY YEARS

Chapter 1

RISING FROM THE ASHES

Once upon a time, when I was still in a crawling stage, I was home alone with my mother. It was lunch-time, and she was preparing food for our family, some corn dough that we call *ubugali* (or *ugali* in Swahili). It is a staple in many parts of Burundi, especially in the high plateau. It goes well with beef stew or just beans mixed with green leafy vegetables, the latter being more affordable.

My mother momentarily left the area where there was a live cooking fire and boiling water, to get the flour in another room, leaving me, the crawling baby, in charge. I crawled after her, obviously not wanting to be left alone. I took the short-cut in her direction, tripping and falling into her pot, three-quarters full of boiling water, which in turn spilled into the live fire, creating enough smoke to burst all smoke alarms (but we had none). And I, the crawling baby, dipped the entire left side of my body: face, arm, leg—into the gleaming fire now doused into hot ashes, thereby burning my small body. I don't know how long I was in those hot ashes, but when my mother returned with her corn flour, she found me grilling to the bone. I can imagine the awful guilt my mom felt when she realized she should have known better than to leave a crawling baby beside a live fire and boiling water.

I was immediately (I hope) rushed to the nearest hospital, about an hour's drive under normal traffic and road conditions, but my parents had no car. They had to walk to that hospital. I learned from my older siblings that my burn was very bad. I was at the hospital close to a year. But time did a good job, and I am happy to report that I fully recovered from the burn trauma and injury. I know I fought for my life with my left hand because that is where I still have scars after all these years. I don't think those scars will ever disappear—a sign forever of how close I came to death. God really spared me that day.

Immediately following my release from the hospital, my mother took me to her parents. Although my stay there was supposed to be temporary, I lived with my maternal grandparents until I finished primary school. In any case, it was like a tradition because all my siblings, except my oldest sister Eugenie, were sent to stay with my grandparents on my mom's side, but only short-term. Only my second oldest sister, Claire, lived there until sixth grade. My two older brothers, Emmanuel and Cyriaque, stayed there a short time and went back to live with my parents when it was time to start school. And here I was, the fifth child. It was my turn to live with Grandpa Bunyoni and my beloved grandmother, Biragumye.

When my grandparents took me in, I was very small and fragile to say the least. When one day, one of my grandmother's best friends saw me, she told her, "My dear friend, although you have been taking care of your daughter's kids, this one is going to be an exception." She implied that I would not make it. My grandmother's feelings were hurt, but Grandma never held a grudge; they remained best friends as long as I can remember. Her friend was like a second grandmother to me, although she wasn't as loving as my beloved Grandmother (*Nyogokuru* in Kirundi). Grandma made it her goal that she would return me to my parents in better shape than she had received me.

Needless to say my grandparents were poor. But since there wasn't any calculated poverty line or threshold at that time, it seemed that poverty wasn't even a word very much known in the villages. My grandmother and my aunts, who lived at home at the time always managed to have something to fill our stomachs. I ate food we grew and I drank fresh banana juice made from the bananas grown on my grandparents' farm. Unless Mother Nature was angry and provided too much or too little rain, we had enough food. At home, I sometimes wore my aunt Aurelia's over-sized shirts, which became dresses for me; and on the first day of school when I started first grade, I wore borrowed clothes from a neighbor's child. So as long as I didn't go without eating for a day, we weren't really poor.

In addition, my grandfather had nearly a hundred cows from when my grandparents first moved to the southern region from the highlands of Bururi province. The southern regions had caused many cattle owners to migrate because they sought greener pastures, which were in abundance in the lower lands and valleys of the country still uninhabited. However, by the time I turned nine or ten years old, we had less than ten cows left. Even though there was rich grass in the lower south, cows didn't tolerate well the summer's heat and humidity. Also, there were too many bugs compared to the hilly landscapes. Therefore, my grandfather's hundred cows had dwindled to ten. Each time a cow was sick, numerous traditional medicines were sought. All of my grandfather's attention was oriented toward his cows. My grandmother did her best to get the cow medicine, which consisted of herbs and other leaves. She tried different kinds to get the cure, but sometimes, she couldn't find the right combination, or she would find it when it was already too late for the cow.

Although life was not easy, we had everything, or I had everything. I had grandparents who loved me unconditionally, cows that filled our compound, and baby cows that occupied half of our house. We had cats too, lots of them. I didn't like them because they slept in my bed, and sometimes, they had babies right there in the corner beside my bed. We didn't know that they triggered my grandmother's asthma attacks. I only have this knowledge now. When I look back, I remember that my grandmother never had a reprieve from her asthma. And since there was a lot of milk, cats always were there, drinking my milk. I didn't like milk, so that was okay—the cats were welcome to drink it all. Grandma tried to force me to drink warm milk fresh out of the cow, but I couldn't. I would take it, go in hiding, and spill it on the dusty floor or in the kitties' milk container. Once in a while, I would drink skim milk.

Skimming, to separate milk from cream, was an elaborate process that used a churn, called *igisabo* in Kirundi. You put milk into the churn, and in a circle motion, you agitated it for about an hour or until the butter granules formed that needed to be separated from the milk. Then you drained the milk into a different container and put the butter in another.

Aging the butter was also a long process that consisted of putting it in a cool dry place in a covered container, and leaving it for months without touching it. When it was considered ripened enough, I remember my grandmother would put a small slice of butter in the food as a condiment; it would melt in, and it was actually yummy! That was the only type of butter my grandmother allowed herself to consume. Because of her health issues, Grandma had limited food choices. So, we used this butter quite often, and my grandfather preferred cow butter to the palm oil that we only used rarely.

At my grandparents' house, my daily chores consisted of fetching cooking wood, carrying water from the river (three miles away), and when I was old enough, leading the cows to the pastures. Once, one of our cows taught me an important lesson about day-dreaming. I must have been on cloud nine when I found myself on top of the cow's horns and up in the air. Usually, when a cow picks you up like that, it shakes you in circular motions and then throws you at a distance. I was afraid of calling for help because I didn't want to make the cow more nervous. Fortunately, before the cow started shaking me on its long horns, a neighbor, who was herding his cows in the same pasture, saw the scene and rushed to save me from the cow. Seeing him come toward it, the cow bent its head and dropped me on the ground. I landed with only minor injuries. That day, I hated cows! I wished them all to be slaughtered right away, so we could eat their meat, and I would be freed from leading them to the pastures. But, of course, no matter what the cows did, my grandfather wasn't going to let that happen. And it's not what I wanted either. If nothing else, I liked our cows for filling our property; they gave me a sense of security, as if the cows were our security guards.

That special cow was a tough one. I remember one time, cow thieves came to my grandparents' farm in the night and stole all our cows, except that one. It had chased them away, and it even woke my grandparents by running around, making noises, pushing the fence, and knocking on the house's door with its horns. That's how we found out that all the cows were gone, except that one. My grandparents called out to neighbors to help and followed in the cows' footprints. Five miles away, the thieves heard the people following in their tracks and calling out, so they gave up and ran into hiding. My grandparents were able to bring our cows back home. It was the scariest night of my youth. Back then, stealing cows was the ultimate threat against cattle owners. Many cattle thieves did it as a lucrative business, and they attempted to steal my grandfather's cows many more times, but the tough cow always chased them away. Sometimes, they would bring salt to tempt the cows to follow them because cows crave salt. But the tough one always kicked them away until eventually they gave up. We named that cow *Bihayi*, "glory".

After my incident with our proud cow Bihayi, I was released from cow herding, leaving that chore to Barenga, my adopted aunt (she had been adopted by my grandparents as a child). My grandma preferred to send me to fetch water and firewood. I liked fetching water better because I could meet other kids my age at the river and play in the water, getting myself wet from head to toe while trying to catch tadpoles. Some of the older girls said that if you got a tadpole to bite your nipples, your breasts would grow instantly. Some of my friends had started growing boobs by then, but I still had a flat chest. So I needed all the help I could get. Despite my efforts, I never caught a tadpole; they're the fastest thing in water.

Some days, I took so long before I brought the water home that my grandma got mad at me because she needed water to start cooking dinner, especially when she was making dry beans that took hours to cook. Because she was unable to pronounce my name correctly, she called me Sakunda instead. "Sakunda, where were you all this time…? Where were you child?" she would demand each time I came back with a bucket half-full of water because I had spilled it all the way home from the river as I tried to rush. She would only yell at me, and she was never upset for more than a minute, letting my grandfather be the bad cop.

Whenever I misbehaved, my grandfather chased me with his walker and hit me with it on my behind, my legs, or even on my head if it were what he could reach. I drove him crazy by running from him and hiding. "Child, come back here! Soon or later I will get you!" Grandpa would threaten because my hiding would work up his anger. And until he had given me a good correction, he never let go. Unlike Grandma, he never let me get away with anything. Even when I hid from him for a day, he would still punish me when I resurfaced. And whenever my grandfather started whipping my behind, my grandmother would defend me, telling him to stop. "Bunyoni, leave that child alone; what will I tell her mother? She entrusted us with that child!" Grandma would say between coughs due to her chronic asthma.

"You tell her that you spoil this child rotten. That's what you will tell her mother or I will!" Grandpa would say.

Although my grandparents never knew it, I was terrified that they would tell my mother I was misbehaving when she would visit us. I prayed that they would forget to tell her about my mischief. And since they were old, I expected them to forget. The idea of telling my mother on me sounded like a way to make me do penance. I had heard my big sister Claire talk about my mother's disciplinarian methods. In those days, hitting a child wasn't considered child abuse; it was tough love. At times, only corporal punishment could reach me and make me behave. Now as a parent myself, I realize that since my grandmother didn't punish me that much, I needed that balance my grandpa provided.

Despite his harsh disciplining, Grandpa loved me, and I still have sweet memories of him. He always gave me leftovers from his food, even when I was full and he wasn't; it was an affectionate gesture, a sign of his love. He was also my favorite story-teller at bedtime. He told me stories of the big-headed monster (*igisizimwe*) that always chased ill-behaved children. The stories didn't actually put me to sleep; they scared me to death and kept me up at night. So, the next day, I would try to behave to avoid meeting the terrifying creature. Grandpa also taught me to pay attention to worldwide news from an early age. He believed that happenings in other parts of the world affected us even in our remote village. He was a news consumer, listening to the radio that his son, my uncle Apollinaire, had given us. And today, knowing what's happening elsewhere in the world keeps me grounded; I attribute that gift to my grandfather.

When my grandparents got older and less mobile, punishment was left mostly to my aunt Aurelia before she got married. She wasn't much of a hitter, but one day, she gave me the lesson of my young life. I was in third grade, and with my best friend Seraphine and my maternal cousin Mediatrice, we started fooling around and getting to school first an hour late, then two hours late.

We would leave home early in the mornings, meet up at our meeting place, and walk slowly, talking and playing games so that we forgot we were going to school. After two or three days of this routine, we eventually started not showing up at all. One day, we were so late that we saw students coming back home after school while we were still on our way. We then turned back and headed home as if we had been in school. Our parents never suspected what we were up to, until a week later when the school summoned them to come and meet our principal and our respective teachers. When the summons was sent home, I instantly knew I was in big trouble. Although Mediatrice and Seraphine were also in trouble, I was the only one not leaving with my "real" parents. I knew that whatever punishment I was in for would be doubled once my mother heard about what I had done.

Aunt Aurelia answered the summons and took me to school that day. After she had been briefed on my case, she went in the nearby bush, cut a fresh switch off a tree, and hid it behind her back. She took me in front of the class, in front of my teacher and my classmates. She whipped my behind and legs, repeating, "*Uzosubire!*" ("If you do that again…!") , which is not a fair translation because when said in Kirundi, it is a real threat! I started to cry. "Swallow your tears!" she said. It wasn't the physical pain that made me cry; it was the humiliation of being beaten in front of the whole class. From that day on, I was a good student and never messed around again.

On another occasion, Aunt Aurelia taught me values through some myths. Early on, I learned a certain myth that palm oil was forbidden to use, a kind of superstition that was believed by cattle owners. For instance, if I ate food with palm oil, I wasn't allowed to drink cow milk, or eat food with cow derived butter. However, sometimes I ate food with palm oil at my friend's house. Then later, I would forget and drink skim milk at home. When I would remember what I had done, I would be so frightened of what would happen to our cows, but I kept silent from fear of repercussions from Grandpa. What if the myths were real and Grandpa's cows got hurt because of what I had done? Grownups told scary stories to children that if we did such things and ate the forbidden food, the cows' udders would fall off. Nothing of the sort happened, of course— at least nothing related to what we ate. So, quite often, I took on the habit of challenging this myth by eating what was forbidden, just to see what would happen.

I was once apprehended eating a fancy donut (called "*mandazi*" in Swahili) that I had been given by one of my friends at school. She was from the Swahili community where they made these donuts to sell. I saved it until I got home and was enjoying it when Aunt Aurelia saw me. "Where did you get that thing?" she quizzed me.

"I got it from my friend Amina at school," I said, my voice shaking in anticipation of her punishment.

"You naughty child," she said, grabbing my arm. "Don't you know you'll cause the cows' udders to fall? Do you want your grandfather to know about this? Why did you eat that kind of food?" Aunt Aurelia demanded.

"But—" I started.

"No buts! Give me that thing." She took the rest of my sweet donut and threw it far into the fields. And then she gave me the spanking of my life. When she was done, I ran and hid for a while. Thank God she didn't tell Grandpa. Even Aurelia was afraid of Grandfather's punishment for me. From then on, I decided that if I ever got a good sweet donut again, I would not show it to anyone. I would finish it at school and come home clean. Those donuts were the sweetest thing I had ever tasted. To this day, I still don't understand the reasons why there were such myths among cattle owners. What I do understand, however, is that drinking milk was a lot healthier for me as a little girl, than eating the *mandazi* full of saturated fats and loaded with sugar. Many such myths were used as a way of teaching good habits and other values to children.

Despite my being sheltered by my grandmother, she couldn't shield me from everything. She had to let the universe take care of me. That is exactly what happened the day she told me to go unleash our calf, which was grazing in the fields, and bring it home. I must have been ten or eleven years old when this happened. The sky had turned gray, and then dark, and seemed bloated and ready to explode. Everyone was in alert mode. I was going to bring the calf home when, all of a sudden, I fell into a ditch and lost consciousness for a few seconds. Then I woke up and smelled this weird smell on me. It was difficult to identify what kind of smell it was. I thought it smelled like something was burning, but I could not quite identify what—maybe burnt plastic. Minutes later, I felt a burn on my left forearm, and I realized I had been struck by lightning, but I was too weak to make any move. I started calling for help, calling my grandma, "Nyogokuru, Nyogo…Grandma…" but my voice was so weak, and in the middle of the thunder and lightning, my voice wasn't loud enough. I waited in the ditch to regain composure and, eventually some strength to call for help. Then I saw another bolt of lightning, followed by the sound of an angry thunder, and my whole body felt like a lifeless mass.

Barenga, my adopted aunt, was calling me and looking for me everywhere. I heard her call my name and I replied, but my voice was too weak for her to hear me. I also heard my grandmother calling my name, "Sakundaaaaa…!" I could hear how anxious her voice was, like she wasn't going to lose me to lightning strikes now when she had already saved my little life once. I remember making the Sign of the Cross in a very grown up way. It was like a knock on God's door, saying, "Please do not let me die and disappoint Grandma." At that very moment, I heard Barenga coming toward me, running frantically. She picked me up from the ditch and brought me in the house. She put me on the floor, and by then, my grandmother was crying nonstop.

The lightning must have really zapped me because my whole body was so weak that it felt like I had no bones, no muscles to put my little body together. My grandmother and Barenga, and whoever else was on the scene, started calling my name to revive me. Their calling went on and on for several minutes. I could hear them, but I felt both present and absent, as if floating in a world I didn't understand, but I wasn't in pain. After a couple of minutes of their calling my name and reviving me, I tried to be strong for Grandma. I wanted to speak, but words wouldn't come out. Then I tried to reassure her with non-verbal communication signs to tell her I was alive but just weak. I wanted to tell Grandma I wasn't dying; that I only needed to sleep, to get a little rest. But Grandma was too anguished to pay attention to what I was trying to communicate. I could tell she had already lost hope that I could survive the lightning strike. I just stayed on that floor, waiting to regain my strength, as I watched her cry endlessly. I don't know what I did after a moment, but it was then that they stopped calling my name. All of a sudden, they relaxed and were relieved that I had made it. I later told my grandmother that it was kind of nice to have a sneak peek to see who would cry if I died. (Naughty child even at my deathbed, huh!)

Whew! There I was, revived and alive, my blood flowing at its normal rate again. I started telling them what had happened, and how God had saved me because I had made the Sign of the Cross. My grandmother started performing some of her traditional medicine on the burn that the lightning had left on my forearm; the very same left arm that had been burnt when I was a crawling baby. It was the only part affected by this tropical storm.

After two weeks, the burn started developing an infection. I went to the dispensary near my school, even though it was believed that only traditional medicine, not modern medicine, should be used in the case of a lightning burn. I went despite my grandmother's pleas never to use modern medicine. I guess I had an attitude at that age, so I would not listen to her. The nurse put some cream on the burn, and it healed the very same week. The clinic staff congratulated me on beating the lightning and staying alive. I still have the scar on my left forearm. Each time I am distraught, I look at it and remember how God again saved me from dying at such a young age.

CHAPTER 1 EVOLVING QUESTIONS FOR REFLECTION

1. What childhood memories do you have that shaped your growing up?

_____

_____

_____

_____

_____

2. What have you learned from those memories that helped/or can help you become a stronger you?

_____

_____

_____

_____

_____

3. Who are the people involved in those memories and how influential were they in your evolvement?

_____

_____

_____

_____

_____

Chapter 2

REFLECTING ON MY ORIGINS

Today you are you! That is truer than true!
There is no one alive who is you-er than you!

— Dr. Seuss

My name is Seconde Nimenya. My last name roughly translates as "only God knows." In my native country of Burundi, many last names include God, especially for Christians. Others, however, reveal how a family copes with life's circumstances. You may hear names with a victory meaning, or names with a victim meaning. My first name, Seconde, however, takes its roots from the Latin name of Secunda. My mother was a fluent reader of the Latin Bible that was introduced in the early nineteenth century into Africa by the Roman Catholic Church. Although my family calls me Sekunda (they dropped the C for the K), in high school, students called me Seconde, and I ended up keeping it that way to make it sound French. Whenever an English speaker asks me my name and I say, "Seconde," pronounced "*Segonde*," they usually hear Sigourney. Maybe I should change it to Sigourney! I've decided that if I ever change my name, it would be fully American with a middle name to boot.

People also like to ask me the meaning of my first name. I usually tell them the meaning in French, which is "second," as in a numerical order. Then they ask whether I am the second-born. Well, I am the fifth out of seven children. As if my name didn't sound mysterious enough, I also have to contend with a mysterious English accent. Each time I talk with an American, I get the compliment that I've come to take for granted. "You have a beautiful accent!"

"Thank you!" I respond. But as much as I enjoy the compliment, I also dread the usual follow up question, "Where are you from?" Then the insecure me thinks, "Gosh, why can't I melt into the crowd and look and speak like Americans instead of always sticking out as an outsider?" I've tried to tell people, "I am Canadian." But for a second, they will ponder my answer, give me a once over, and not be easily fooled. So, next comes, "But where do you come from originally?" with a fat emphasis on originally. At this point, I can't continue to fake my origins. I didn't actually know I had been playing this game until my two teenage daughters once sat me down, and said "Mom, we've noticed that each time someone asks you where you come from, you lie!" Gee, thanks girls. I might have wanted to fake my origins for reasons that are not obvious to most Americans. Coming from a country that's known for being war-torn and makes the list of poorest in the world every year, I thought that maybe if I just forgot about it, and focused on being my adoptive country's full citizen, it would lessen the pain I feel about my native country.

Since I now live here in the beautiful United States of America, I have started considering that people's questions might be well intended. They want to get to know me and my origins, and maybe they want to connect with me. Most want to learn something new by asking questions about places they've never been. When I let my guard down and say, "I come from Burundi," we get to another level of questions, and this time, I feel compelled to explain where my homeland is located. Depending on people's interest, I throw in a little bit of history and even politics. Sometimes, people ask me, "Is Burundi an exotic island?" No, it's not an island, but it has the same kind of beauty as any exotic place.

I don't think many folks here in America know that Burundi is even a country. Sometimes even I have a hard time finding it on the African map. It looks like a dot, a little drop in a big ocean, as Burundian singers so eloquently used to put it. When she was in middle school, my middle child Elva told me that she had been taught about Africa in social studies. "That's a good thing, sweetie!" I said proudly. But then Elva said, "It's so boring Mom; we can't wait for this subject to be over!" I bet it was boring. It bored me too when I was in high school learning about those weird names of old African tribes. What teenager in his or her right mind needs to learn about the *Mossi* Empire or the *Mandingue* tribe? We were also asked to memorize country capitals in a song (and that's how I still remember a couple of them), presidents around the world, and all Burundi's government ministers and other high ranking politicians' names. At every *coup d'état* or reelection, they changed them, and we had to start all over again.

It was only after I was grown that I realized what a wealth of knowledge I had about the world in general. So, I told Elva that she should strive to learn about Africa because it's the second largest continent both in area and population, but its history is the least known. My husband, Claver, who is also from Burundi, told me a story about when he first arrived in Canada. He rode a bus from Mirabel airport in Montreal to Sherbrooke, where he was going to study for his master's degree. On the bus, he met a passenger, and they started chatting.

"Where are you from?" the passenger asked him.

"I come from Burundi," Claver told him.

"Where is that?" the passenger asked.

"It's in Africa," my husband informed the man.

"Do you guys have houses in Africa?" the passenger asked, really wanting to know.

"Oh, no! We live in trees. As a matter of fact, your ambassador lives in the biggest tree because he has an important job," Claver answered. The passenger didn't reply; and I'm not sure he understood that Claver was only joking.

Because of such situations, I was excited when my daughter said they were learning about Africa in social studies; it's the only way to shed some light on the continent, one country at a time.

Burundi is a small landlocked country located in East-Central Africa. It is bordered by Rwanda on the north, the Democratic Republic of Congo on the west, and Tanzania on the east. It covers only 10,745 square miles with a population of 10,557,259 according to a 2012 estimate. Burundi's capital and largest city is Bujumbura. Kirundi and French are its two official languages. Swahili is spoken mainly in Bujumbura and other commercial centers, and it is often a language of communication between Burundians and their eastern counterparts, such as Tanzanians and Kenyans. The weather is temperate;

only Bujumbura, located alongside Lake Tanganyika, is hot and humid. When it comes to the climate, Burundi is a paradise on Earth. Its evergreen forests, mild temperatures, lakes, exotic birds, and endless pastures offer an enjoyable panorama that has long been the envy of Westerners.

Many foreigners adore Burundi. I met an American man on the plane when I went to visit my family in 2006 who was working for the United Nations on a reconstruction mission in Burundi. He was in his late fifties, tanned by the zenith sun, and had a thick goatee.

"Do you like it in Burundi?" I asked him.

"I have fallen in love with Burundi. Out of all the underdeveloped countries I have been assigned to, Burundi is by far the best place," he said, adding that the people were cheerful despite their problems and poverty. He found the weather to be clement, and he said to be there was an indulgence for a Westerner used to rough winters.

"That's true," I nodded. I used to think there was no better place to live on Earth before I left Burundi in 1992. When I was a little girl living with my grandparents, I recall running outside, basking in the sun, especially in the summer months. I would pirouette to let the wind lift up my skirts to show off my underwear when I started wearing them in first grade.

After we landed at the Bujumbura airport, I saw my American acquaintance kissing a girl who had come to welcome him. On my way back to America, we met again, and while waiting for our connecting flight at the Addis Ababa International Airport in Ethiopia, I saw him hugging and then kissing this cute Ethiopian girl. No wonder he liked it out there; he had wonderful UN benefits!

My hometown is in southern Burundi, in the province of Makamba. My parents have always lived in Vugizo, a small town in the southwest of the province. Vugizo's nickname is "la Suisse" because of its landscape similarities with Switzerland. It is a high rough plateau on the side of a group of mountains, Mount Inanzegwe being the highest in the region at 7064 feet elevation. The climate in Vugizo is also a little chillier than in the lower landscapes of the rest of Makamba. It rains a lot during rainy season (December to April) and is often foggier in Vugizo than in the rest of the province. It is windy and dry during the dry season (July to August). The months of September to November are called small wet season because it rains, but not as heavily as the rainy season months. Also, the months of May to June are called the small dry season, as it is dry but not as dry as the months of July and August.

My hometown's main challenge is the lack of good roads due to its geographic landscape. Because of the rough mountains and hillsides surrounding the town, it has always been difficult for the government to build decent roads. There is only one road that connects to Vugizo, no matter what direction you are coming from. Students from other parts of the country used to tease Vugizo natives about there being only one road, "the road to Vugizo." You have to take other major roads that go to the city of Makamba's city center, and then take the connecting road from there to Vugizo—a bumpy ride to say the least. So much for being like Switzerland! But during my university years in the capital, I was always excited whenever I reached that bumpy road when I went to visit my parents. The landscape—mountains and endless hills—is breathtaking. It felt like home to me, and I wouldn't have traded it for any other place.

But the last time I visited my parents, I complained a lot about the road's conditions. After almost fifteen years of enjoying the comfort of North American roads and highways, I felt discomfort on the bumpy road. Those who were traveling with me kept apologizing for the road's conditions, as if it were their fault. They also asked me to compare the road to the ones in America. Well, where should I have begun? Should I have described all the interstates? How about the beautiful bridges? But I knew what their questions implied. How could this tiny country, their beloved Burundi, not have decent roads, when big countries like Canada or the United States have all those highways and bridges? I simply told them that it was impossible to compare Burundi to the U.S. or Canada because of their differences in economic development.

Fortunately, the bumpy road is only an hour's drive, and before I knew it, we were at my parents' home. My son Darrel, who was with me on that trip, was so amazed by what he saw that he still talks about it with awe to his sisters. For him, seeing cows, chickens, and goats, up close and personal, was the most amazing experience he had ever had. And I was happy that, at six years old, he got to experience the difference between his life in North America and life in Burundi. He had a blast and appreciated everything he saw. Darrel amazed me with how he adapted to the people he was seeing for the first time. I especially loved seeing him bond with my mother, even though he didn't speak Kirundi, and she was unable to speak English or French. But the two communicated their love through a non-verbal language, and wherever my mother went, Darrel followed. To me, this was a testimony that love truly doesn't speak any language because love is the language.

My son took every opportunity to run outside and play without the restrictions I put on him when we are in America. He felt free to talk to strangers for no particular reason. He actually thought anyone who was black was related to us. In my hometown, my son and I were special guests. All my neighbors came to welcome us, and they even danced for us till the wee hours. I was amused by one of my neighbors, a man in his late seventies, who knows a thing or two about riches. He asked me, "So, tell me my child, I hear America is beautiful. Is it true that it's sparkling, and has marble everywhere you go?"

"Oh yes, marble is everywhere!" I said. I couldn't bring myself to spoil his enthusiasm and knowledge about America. In another instance, Darrel was the one particularly impressed. On our way back to Bujumbura from my parents' house, we met school kids in their khaki uniforms, going back home. It was a wet day. It had been raining for three steady consecutive days. This was February, the middle of the rainy season. Our pickup truck got stuck in the mud, and couldn't move. Some of the kids were my son's age, if not younger. But, they climbed the pickup truck as it kept sliding in the mud, and moving in spirals. One of the kids yelled at our driver, "You don't know how to drive? Pass me the wheel!" Despite their apparent poverty, these kids seemed happy, loud, and free to be just kids. Most of them do not get to see cars up-close often, which is why they came to our spiraling pickup to experience the spectacle when they saw it moving slowly. The driver had to chase them away to get them off the vehicle, and they ran giggling.

Those kids reminded me of my elementary school years, those early times when I would walk two hours to go to school with my big sister Claire yelling at me because I wasn't fast enough. Some days, I just couldn't take it anymore, so I would drop on the ground crying. Claire would grab my hand, and literally drag me behind her. Back in those days, schools were only found at major commercial centers, where Arabic merchants had established Swahili communities before the colonization by Germany and then Belgium in the early twentieth century. The colonizers had then built schools following in the steps of those commercial centers. When I was in elementary school, it was very common in many parts of the country only to have one primary school within twenty to thirty miles, and we had no school buses. Nowadays, they have elementary schools located within as little as five miles walking distance, something I never thought would be possible in my lifetime.

CHAPTER 2 EVOLVING QUESTIONS FOR REFLECTION

1. Take a moment to reflect on your roots; do you know your origins?

_____

_____

_____

_____

_____

2. Was there a time when you had mixed or conflicting feelings about your origins?

_____

_____

_____

_____

_____

3. If so, what did those feelings and emotions ignite in you?

_____

_____

_____

_____

_____

18 LESSONS I WISH MY MOTHER HAD TAUGHT ME

1. **Owning your own happiness**: Do not fall into the trap of thinking that someone else is responsible for making you happy; others can contribute to making you happier, but you have to own your happiness first.

2. **Loving from within**: You cannot give what you don't have. It is by loving yourself that you can begin to love others.

3. **Getting a good education**: Nothing can substitute for a good education; it opens doors for you to use your God-given talents.

4. **Carving out financial stability**: Buy assets if you can afford to, or save money until you are clear what kind of assets you want to acquire. Invest in your retirement fund before and after you get married. If you get married and have to stay home to take care of your children and family, ask your spouse to set up a savings account in your name, and save every month. Please understand that this account is not to

pay you for taking care of your family. No one can ever pay you enough for parenthood. This account is to allow you to buy underwear without having to ask for permission.

5. **Attracting the one**: Stay away from relationships that are abusive in any manner: verbal, physical, or emotional. When dating, spend some time getting to know each other before merging your lives. It is godly to choose a partner who is nice to you. Role-play your marriage before you are married to see how you and your future spouse will respond to real life circumstances. Analyze how as a couple you complement each other's personality traits. Be yourself and don't play a character, falling into the trap of unleashing the real you after your "I do's". Give each other a chance to know who you are as a person from the start.

6. **Knowing yourself**: Know what you value in a relationship. If the relationship is built on things that you value such as honesty, trust, and respect, it won't take too much "remodeling," only simple adjustments.

For the full list of lessons, read
Evolving Through Adversity - See the following
Information and Links.

ABOUT THE AUTHOR

Seconde Nimenya is a diversity leader and an international award-winning author of ***Evolving Through Adversity***, a story of her life journey in which she shares the life lessons she has learned along the way to inspire others. Her second book, ***A Hand to Hold*** is an inspirational novel of love, healing and redemption. And her third book, ***A Leader's Companion Workbook to Evolving Through Adversity*** is filled with leadership insights for personal and professional development.

Seconde is the Founder of COMMON PURPOSE TRAINING SERVICES **(CPTS),** and serves as CPTS's Principal Diversity Leadership Trainer for clients ranging from small to large organizations and world-class universities and colleges. She helps leaders and employees achieve cultural transformations, develop cultural competence and engage a diverse workforce, while bridging the gaps between diverse and multicultural communities both locally and globally. Her expertise is in debunking diversity stereotypes and biases that affect the workplace from attracting, hiring and retaining a diverse workforce.

Seconde holds a bachelor's degree in history, a bachelor's degree in business administration with a major in finance and an MBA. She blends her varied cultural and educational backgrounds to create dynamic presentations, using a unique approach that is both inspiring and empowering. She is a firm believer that despite our social identities such as race, gender, ethnicity, religion and sexual orientation, we are far more alike than we are different. She advocates for diversity and inclusion in the workplace and the educational systems, as well as raises key global issues such as the violence against women, child marriage and education for girls.

Her TED Talk on Race and other Identity Constructs, titled, *"We Are Not All That Different"* has been hailed as the most inspirational TED Talk for our times. As a frequent keynote speaker, trainer and advocate, Seconde inspires people on how to bridge the gaps between diverse and multicultural communities. In 2017, Seconde was honored with **"The Seeds Of Hope Award,"** recognizing her contributions in bridging the gaps between our diverse and multicultural communities. For more information about her work, visit: www.SecondeNimenya.com

BOOK SECONDE NIMENYA
to speak at your next event

Using thought-provoking and powerful principles, Seconde Nimenya's presentations will impact how your teams interact at work and in life; getting them to think in new and creative ways. Her topics work well as Keynotes, Workshops or Seminars.

Seconde's presentations entertain as they educate, leaving your audience wanting more out of life and work!

CONTACT INFORMATION
Email to: info@SecondeNimenya.com
Website: www.SecondeNimenya.com

Also by Seconde Nimenya

Available in Paperback,
eBook and Audiobook
wherever books are sold,
and SecondeNimenya.com

www.ingramcontent.com/pod-product-compliance
Lightning Source LLC
Chambersburg PA
CBHW051650260626
47170CB00004B/1420